Blooming Love
A collection of two different romances

Blooming Love

Skye Rickman

Published by Skye Rickman, 2024.

BLOOMING LOVE

First edition. June 22, 2024.

ISBN: 979-8227527325

Written by Skye Rickman.

You are about to read two different romances. The first one is The Magic Academy. Lilly is a talented Witch who is about to graduate from the prestigious Magic Academy. That is until she catches the attention of a infamous dark wizard. Will he pull her into the darkness or will she find love with her favourite teacher?

THE SECOND STORY IS Darkness Falls. It's a rockstar romance about a girl named Lila. She had been abused her whole life by everyone she ended up dating. That is until she fell in love with someone that would change her life forever.

Meet the characters of The Magic Academy

LILLY - 16 YEAR OLD witch with alot of potential. She has blue eyes and dark brown hair. She loves the color pink and styling herself with bows.

Rose - 16 year old witch with a talent for potions. She is Lilly's best friend. She has blonde hair and green eyes. She loves everything light blue.

Alan - 45 years old. Lilly's dad and teacher of the dark arts. He is the leader of Drake's army. He has shoulder length black hair and brown eyes. He will do anything to protect his daughter.

Drake - 47 years old. A powerful dark wizard that Alan works for . He has short black hair and blue eyes. Very handsome but dangerous.

Skylar - 16 year old witch that hates Lilly and is always out to get her. She has long dark red hair and brown eyes.

Emma - 40 year old potions teacher. She is a bit weird but most people enjoy her class. She has long messy brown hair and blue eyes.

Morse - 55 years old. He is the school headmaster. He is kind but don't get on his bad side. He has white hair down to his shoulders and purple eyes. A witch cursed him years ago which changed his eye color.

Sirus - 45 years old spell master. He teaches the students spells they can use in their everyday life. He has shoulder length brown hair and green eyes. He is kind but to a point.

Lanex - 17 year old wizard. He is a minor character that only causes trouble. He has short blonde hair and blue eyes.

Ps there will also be one or two mystery characters. Also age of consent for dating is 16.

Chapter 1: First day of Senior Year

Lilly just reached her new dorm for her final year at the academy. Her dad pulled some strings and got her a room by herself. He helped her carry her luggage into her room. "Thanks dad." She said giving him a hug and a kiss. "Your welcome sweetie. I hope you have a wonderful day."

He left her to unpack. She began decorating her room. She put pink sheets on her bed and some fluffy pillows. She put a vase of pretty roses on the window sill. She put her clothes away in the closet and put her jewelry box on a desk. It was a wooden jewelry box with a butterfly painted on it. Her mother gave it to her before she passed away.

She put a picture of her and her parents on the desk. Then she gathered her books and put them in her pink messenger bag. She loved everything pink. Since It was the first day there were no classes. She headed to her dad's office. He worked for a wizard who's identity was unknown to her. His office was part of his boss's office building which was off campus.

She had to step into a portal and chant where she wanted to go. "Lux offices." She chanted. Suddenly she was transported there. The doorman greeted her. "Good morning Lilly go on in." He said smiling . She smiled back and walked in. The office was always filled with mysterious looking people but she paid them no mind. She took the elevator up to the sixth floor. There was two offices. Her dad's and someone named Drake.

She looked around and her dad wasn't there. She decided to put her books down and open her spell book. She took out her wand. It was a gorgeous shade of dark purple with roses engraved on it. She began chanting a levitating spell. She tried to lift her book off the desk. Her book started lifting up and she was getting excited. Suddenly she heard someone behind her. She jumped and dropped her book. "Don't be scared. I'm Drake. Your dad's boss." He said, smiling at her. "Oh ok hello." She said blushing. He was quite handsome. "Let me help you." He said as he slowly put his hand on hers. She started shaking a little. "Don't be afraid." He whispered in her ear . It sent chills down her spine. She chanted the spell and the book floated up to the ceiling as he guided her hand. Then it came back down.

"See, you are a natural." He said as he took his hand off hers. "Your dad should be returning soon. I hope I see you again. You are very pretty. " He said, putting his lips on her hand to give her a kiss. Then he wrote his number in her notebook. He walked back to his office. Her heart was fluttering. She has never been in love before but this wizard was different.

Her dad got off the elevator and greeted her with a hug and kiss. "Why aren't you at the academy?" He asked. "There are no classes today dad." Drake was looking at her from his office window. When he caught Alan's eye, he looked away. He walked over to him. "Did you talk to my daughter?" He asked angerly. "So what if I did? I'm your boss I can do whatever I want. "Stay away from her." Warned Alan. Drake stood up from his desk and got in his face. "If you want to keep your job I suggest you leave me alone." Said Drake. With that he went back in his office, and locked the door.

"Please stay away from him. He's not a good person." "Don't worry dad, I have no interest in him." She said reassuring him. "Please don't come here unless it's with me. Just in case ok?" "Dad I'm in advanced classes. I think I can handle myself. I will be careful though." She said hugging him. "I love you so much. Why don't we go back to school. It's almost dinner time." Said Alan smiling. They went back down the elevator and headed towards the portals. She held her dad's hand and chanted "The Magic Academy." They appeared at the school doors in an instant.

Back at Drake's office he pulled out a jewelry box with a gold flower necklace. This was no ordinary necklace. He wrote a note to put inside the box.

Meeting you was the best day of my life

I hope to call you mine someday

My sweet Lilly

He wrapped up the box in pretty gold wrapping paper.

Rose, Lilly's BFF ran up and hugged her. "I'll let you two catch up." "Bye dad." she said smiling. "Are you excited for senior year?" asked Rose. "Yes I can't wait to graduate." "Do you know who you are going to ask to prom?" "I'll probably go alone, I don't like anyone that way." Replied Lilly. "I don't know who to ask either. I know it will be fun though whether we have dates or not." "What classes do you have?" "Just potions and spells because I took extra classes next year." Replied Lilly. "I should have done that. I have everything." "You will be fine. At least we graduate together." Said Lilly.

"Let's get to the dining hall. It's almost dinner time." Said Rose as she grabbed Lilly by the hand and ran down the hall. Meanwhile Alan approached a boy named James. "Can you ask my daughter Lilly to prom? She is interested in someone that is no good for her and I want to find her a distraction." "I can for a price. Give me 50 in gold coin." Said James. "Deal." Replied Alan as he slipped the coin in his hand. "Make up some story like you have liked her for a while and here give her these flowers." "Ok." Replied James.

Alan headed to the dining hall, keeping a distance from James. Lilly and Rose were already there sitting down together. James got into the dining hall and Alan soon got there too. James walked up to Lilly and handed her the flowers. "Lilly I have liked you for awhile and I was wondering if you would go to prom with me?" "I don't know you very well but ok I will." Replied Lilly. Alan snapped a photo of them with his phone. "Great I'll meet you there around 7." He said then he walked to sit down with his friends.

"Now I just need a date." "You will find one. You are so pretty." Said Lilly. Rose smiled at her. They started bringing dinner out. Yummy pizza.

Alan took the elevator up to his office. Drake was there working on some paperwork. He sent the picture to Drake's phone of Lilly and James. As soon as he looked at it, he stormed out of his office. "Now you can leave my daughter alone. She has a boy interested in her." You don't tell me what to do. If I want Lilly I will have her. Don't cross me again or I will take more then your job." Warned Drake.

Chapter 2: Drake

LILLY WOKE UP WITH a text from an unknown number. "I don't want to get you in trouble but it's me Drake. I know your father doesn't like me but I hope I can see you again." Lilly started typing back. "I've never had a boyfriend before but I want to see you too and get to know you more. Can we meet somewhere after school?" "Yes we can I'll figure something out. I hope you have a wonderful day ◈" She typed back with a ☺" emoji.

She began getting dressed in her school uniform. It was a black and blue checkered dress and flat black shoes. She put her hair up in a ponytail and applied some pink lipstick. Then she straightened up her bed.

She then left her room and locked her door. She started walking to potions class. The school was huge but she knew her way around. She found a seat next to rose and they hugged eachother. She loved Emma, the teacher. She was a weird but funny. Her hair was always wild and curly. She always made the class fun. "Today we will be making a healing potion. If you are injured in anyway and need a quick recovery, this is perfect." She said getting out the ingredients. "It contains dragons blood, witches warts, troll hair, and peppermint oil. I've written the directions on the board. You may partner up and begin brewing your potions.

Lilly and Rose started working on the potion together.

Two drops of dragons blood. Two witches warts. A fistful of troll hair and three drops of peppermint oil. They mixed their ingredients into the cauldron that had water already in it. It fizzed and turned purple. Professor Emma walked around to acess how everyone was doing. She went up to Lilly and looked in the cauldron. "Well done girls. You get an A for today. " She said smiling at them. "Everyone did ok for today." Soon class was over. It seemed to fly by.

"I got to go to herbology class but I'll see you later." "Ok see you." Replied Lilly. She began walking back to her room for her break period. Her phone started ringing. It was Drake. "Hey how are you?" She asked him. "I'm doing better now that I get to talk to you. Do you want to go to dinner with me tonight? I rented out the Witches Brew so it will be just us."

"Yes I'd love to. How about 6? "That's perfect. I got you a dress for our date. I didn't know your size but it's a magical dress so it will conform to your body. My assistant should be dropping it off to the school shortly." Said Drake. "You didn't have to do that." "Id do anything for you. I'll see you soon." He replied. Then he hung up.

Lilly reached her room but before she could get in her door she was stopped by Skylar and Lanex. "What do you want?" She asked them. Lanex pressed himself against her. "I want you." He replied as he tried to grab her butt and kiss her. She tried to push him off of her but he pinned her against the door. She tried to scream but he covered her mouth. Sirus the spell teacher came around the corner and saw what was going on. He cast a spell paralyzing Lanex and he fell to the floor. "You can't do that he's a student!" Screamed Skylar. Sirus held unto Lilly and they teleported to his office. He locked the door.

Lilly started crying. She hugged him and cried into his chest. He wrapped his arms around her. "It will be ok Lilly. I'll make sure he doesnt hurt you again." He said kissing the top of her head. She looked up at him surprised. "I'm sorry if that was inappropriate. I won't do it again. She reached up and kissed him on the cheek. "Thank you for saving me." "May I give you my number. Just in case you need me again? Just don't tell anyone." said Sirus. "Yes, go ahead." So Sirus put his number in her phone. "I'm going to get you back to your room. Keep your door locked until your dad or I get you. I'll let him know what happened." He teleported her back to her room.

She locked the door quickly. She hugged him again. "Thank you for everything." "No problem Lilly. I'm going to get a hold of your dad. Then I'll come get you." Said Sirus then he teleported.

A few minutes went past and there was a knock at her door. "Who is it?" "I'm Richard, Drake's assistant." He answered. She carefully opened her door. There stood a tall muscular man, with short black hair and blue eyes. He was dressed in a black suit and tie. He handed her a beautiful pink sequin dress. "Thank you so much." "Your welcome. Drake is very excited to see you." He teleported himself back to Drake's office. Lilly went back in and locked her door.

"Boss it looked like she had been crying and she seemed shaken up." "I will find out what happened when I see her tonight." Replied Drake.

Lilly got another knock on her door. "Honey it's dad." She opened her door and gave him a big hug. "That jerk is suspended. So you don't need to worry about him." "Thank you dad I love you." Love you too sweetie." He replied kissing her cheek. "Sirus is going to take you to class so no one bothers you." "Ok dad." She replied. "I'll see you later honey." Said Alan as he walked away.

"You can sit out today if you want to. Since you have been through a lot." "Ok I think I will. Thank you." She replied smiling at him. They walked to class together. A few kids were already there. Rose ran and hugged her. "I'm so sorry I heard what happened. "I'm ok thanks to Sirus. I'm so grateful he was there." Replied Lilly as she smiled at him.

"I'm going to sit out today though." "I don't blame you." replied Rose. Soon everyone got there. "Today we will be learning defensive spells. Everyone partner up except Lilly." Said Sirus. "Oh so you defend her and now she doesn't need to participate in class. I'm going to spread a rumor that you two are dating and get you fired." Said Skylar.

"Your friend tried to assault her so I suggest you shut your mouth or I will give you detention." He said sternly. "Now pair up and practice casting defensive spells please." Everyone got together while Lilly watched.

Sirus texted Lilly while he watched the other students. Some were struggling but Rose and a few other students were doing well. "We have to be careful that we are not seen together because of Skylar. Hopefully she does not spread a rumor though." "I understand I will be careful. Thank you for being there for me ☺ " Typed Lilly. "☺" He typed back. She blushed .

Soon class was over. Rose joined Lilly as they walked to the dining hall for dinner. She didn't want her dad to know she had a dinner date so she planned on just eating a little. She sat down and nibbled on her spaghetti. Her dad walked up to her. "Are you ok baby? You are not eating much." "I'm just not hungry dad. I'm still shook up." She replied. "Dont worry honey. Sirus and I will keep an eye on you. Nothing like that will ever happen again. "Thank you dad I love you." She said hugging him. "Love you too sweetie. I'll see you later." He said as he walked away.

"I'm here for you too." Said Rose and she hugged her. Lilly smiled. They soon finished eating. "I'll see you tomorrow." "Bye Rose." Replied Lilly. Lilly started making her way to the portals. She stepped in one and chanted "Witches Brew". She was suddenly transported in front of the restaurant. She cast a spell on herself changing from her school clothes into her new dress. It was amazing what you could do with magic.

She was greeted at the front door by Richard. He held the door for her. She walked into a beautifully decorated restaurant. Drake stood up and walked over to her. He was dressed in a sharp dark blue suit. He hugged her and kissed her in the cheek. "You look so beautiful. I'm glad you came." "You are so handsome." She replied.

"Please sit down." He said as he pulled the chair out for her. She sat down and smiled at him as he sat across from her. "For you." He said as he handed her a gift box. "Thank you but you didn't have to." Said Lilly. "Yes I do, anything for my future girlfriend."

She opened the box and her mouth dropped when she saw the necklace. "This is beautiful." She said putting it on. "That necklace is special. If you are attacked it is embedded with magic that will make almost any attack bounce off you. Make sure you are wearing it all times." "Ok I will." She replied. The waiter suddenly walked up to them. "Are you ready to order?" "Yes I'll have the chicken Parm." "and for the gentleman?" "I'll have the steak and bring two glasses of your finest wine." Replied Drake. The waiter went off into the kitchen.

"I'm not old enough to drink." "You are if you are in the company of an older adult that is going to take care of you." He said while winking at her. "Ok I trust you." He reached his hand across the table to hold hers. "I have a question to ask you. What happened at school today? When my assistant dropped off your dress, he said you looked upset."

Lilly started tearing up. "A boy tried to grab me innapropraitly at school. A teacher stopped him through so I'm ok. He got up from the table and held her tight. "What was this jerks name?" "Lanex." Answered Lilly as she cried in his chest. He ran his fingers through her hair. "I will make sure no one ever hurts you again. I know that we can't legally date until you are 17 but I will still be here for you." Thank you." She replied.

They sat back down together. Soon the food and the wine arrived. Lilly took a bite of her food. "This is so delicious." "I'm glad you like it." Replied Drake. She took a sip of her wine. "Wow that's good but strong." Said Lilly. "You will get used to it. I'm hoping we can go on a few dates a week." "I'd like that." Replied Lilly. They soon finished their meal.

The waiter came to collect the tab and Drake put down a hundred dollar tip like it was nothing. He held Lilly in his arms and kissed her on the cheek. She kissed him back. "I'm going to cast a spell sending you straight to your room so that you won't get in trouble. Thank you for a wonderful night." "Thank you." Replied Lilly as she smiled at him.

He waved his wand and suddenly she was back in her room. There was flowers and chocolates waiting for her on her desk. The note attached read : I know this may be wrong because I'm your teacher but I think I'm falling for you. After you graduate, can you give me a chance? – Sirus. Lilly texted Sirus. "I got your gift. The flowers smell beautiful and the chocolates look yummy. Thank you." Sirus smiled as he texted back. "What do you think about what I said?" "if I'm single when I graduate I'm all yours." She typed back. She likes Drake too so she tried to be indirect with her response. "Sounds wonderful. I wish you were graduated though so we could go on a date." Lilly is falling for Drake but she likes Sirus too and doesn't want to hurt him. "I wish we could too." she replied. "I'll let you get some sleep goodnight sweet Lilly." "Goodnight Sirus."

Chapter 3: Date Night

Lilly woke up to a text from Drake. "Good morning my beautiful Lilly I hope you have a wonderful day." "Good morning I hope you have a great day." She texted back. She then got herself ready for the day. She heard a knock at her door. "It's just me." Said Sirus. She opened her door and locked it behind her. "Your not worried that Skylar will spread rumors about us?"

"I already told your dad and Morse her intentions and they are not going to listen to her. Besides it's not like we will be holding hands down the hall." Said Sirus smiling at her. So they walked together to the dining hall for breakfast. Sirus went and sat next to Morse and Lilly sat next to Rose. Lilly hid Drake's necklace under her shirt so no one would see.

"A few more days till prom. Are you excited for your date? "I'm not really interested in him anymore. I'll go on the date out of sympathy but that's it. Don't tell anyone but I like an older man." "I won't say anything." Said Rose. "We need to go pick out our dresses." She continued. "We can go shopping at the "Magic Wardrobe." Said Lilly.

Soon their breakfast came. Hot coco, waffles and bacon. It was Lilly's favorite. She suddenly got a text. "You are cute when you eat." Said Sirus. Lilly smiled and typed back. "You make me smile." She

said while smiling at him. Rose caught her looking at him. "It's professor Sirus isn't it?" "Shhh." Said Lilly.

Alan caught Sirus looking at Lilly. He whispered to him "Are you interested in my daughter?" "I'm sorry Alan, I won't look at her." Replied Sirus. "You have my blessing to date her when she graduates. My boss has an interest in her so I already paid a boy to ask her to prom because I want to keep her away from him." "I will take good care of her I promise." Said Sirus. "I know you will."

They soon finished eating and it was time to go to spell class. Lilly and Rose walked together to class. Sirus caught up to them. "Lilly may I talk to you for a minute?" He asked. They went to the corner of the classroom. Sirus whispered "Your dad caught me looking at you and gave me permission to date you. He said he wants you to stay away from his boss." "Ok when do you want to go on our first date?" Asked Lilly. "I don't know but we need to keep it a secret for now. I wish I could kiss you." "Me too." Replied Lilly.

Soon everyone arrived for class. Everyone paired up. "Today is simple. We are going to practice healing spells." said Sirus. "Since no one is hurt, if the spell is done correctly you should just feel better if it works." He continued. Rose cast a spell on Lilly. She felt a little better. Lilly did the same to her. She felt a lot better. "Good job girls." "Everyone is doing good." Said Sirus. Everyone practiced till class was over.

Lilly left last and winked at Sirus. He smiled and winked back. Lilly began walking back to her room for her free period. Her dad caught up to her. "Hi sweetie." "Hi dad." "Tonight I want to give you and Sirus a date night in my office at school so you too can get to know eachother." "Really? thank you Dad." She said hugging him. "You need to start distancing yourself from Drake though, but he has a temper. So start seeing him less and less. Eventually not at all. I need to tell you something else too. I hired James to take you to prom. I've already told him the deal is off. I did it to keep you from Drake. I'm sorry." "It's ok dad. I really like Sirus anyway. Thank you for everything dad, I love you." She said hugging him. "I love you too. I'll see you later."

She got in her room but didn't lock the door. Suddenly her phone started ringing. It was Drake. "Hi beautiful how are you doing?" "I'm good how are you?" She replied. "I'm good I was wondering if you want to go on another date tomorrow night." "Id love to." "That's wonderful.

I can't wait to see you. I'll talk to you later bye honey." "Bye handsome." She replied.

There was a knock at her door. "Hey!" She said excitedly. "Come in." Sirus came in and she shut and locked the door. "My dad is setting up a date night for us tonight." "I know I can't wait." He said wrapping his arms around her. "I can't stay because I have another class but I wanted to see you." He leaned in to give her their first kiss together. "Wow, I've never had a kiss before. That was amazing. " Said Lilly. "That was my first too. I've never even had a girlfriend." "Really? Well I can't wait to be your girlfriend." "I can't wait to be your boyfriend." He said kissing her again.

"Ok I gotta go before we get caught. I'll see you later." He said as he teleported away. A few hours went by and it was time for dinner. Lilly left her room and Rose was waiting for her. "Hey bestie how was your day?" "It was great I have a date tonight but don't tell anyone." Said Lilly. "Ok I won't. Are you excited to go dress shopping tomorrow?" "Yes I can't wait!" Said Lilly excitedly.

They sat down together. It was spaghetti and meatballs tonight. Alan whispered in Sirus ear. "I got my office ready for you. You and Lilly can watch a movie together. Don't get handsy with her." He said sternly. "I won't I promise."

Sirus looked at Lilly and smiled at her. She realized she had suace on her chin. She wiped it off and blushed. Sirus giggled. Soon they finished eating. She hugged Rose. "See you tomorrow." "See you." Said Rose. Lilly headed to her Dad's office. Sirus and Alan were already there. "Hi honey." He said hugging her. "Hi dad." "Remember to keep this door locked. I have a key. I will come get you when it's late." "Thank you so much dad." "Your welcome sweetie love you." "Love you too." Alan left.

Alan set up a couch and a TV for them . There was also sparkling water and popcorn. Sirus wrapped his arms around her and kissed her. Then they sat on the couch together. Sirus poured her some water and then grabbed the fresh popcorn. He snapped his fingers and a blanket appeared over them. "What do you want to watch?" "It doesn't matter. I'm just happy to be here with you." She said smiling. "Ok I'll find a comedy or something."

Lilly lays her head on his chest. She feels safe with him. He kisses the top of her head. He finds a movie and wraps his arms around her . They nibble on some popcorn while they snuggle together. Soon they were laughing and stealing kisses between eachother. Lilly started getting tired and fell asleep in his arms. Sirus turned the volume down and put the popcorn and drinks on the table. He shut his eyes and drifted to sleep.

An hour or so later Alan unlocked the door. Sirus woke up but Lilly was still sleeping. "Did you both have a good time?" "Yes Alan we did. I'm falling in love with her. I don't want to tell her too soon though and scare her away." Said Sirus. "Her 17 th birthday is coming up soon and graduation. I would tell her close to then. Once she's graduated you two won't get in trouble." "Good idea." He said as he kissed her on her forehead. "Wake up sweetie it's time for bed." Said Sirus. Lilly woke up and kissed Sirus on the lips. He kissed her back softly.

"Honey we got to get you to bed. I'll teleport you there." "Ok dad I love you. See you soon Sirus." "See you soon Lilly." He replied. Alan waved his wand and sent Lilly back to her room. "I hope to marry your daughter some day." "You have my blessing Sirus."

Chapter 4: Falling For Them

Lilly woke up excited to go shopping for prom. She woke up to texts from Drake and Sirus. Drake said "I can't wait for our date tonight. Meet me at my office at 7. I will have a surprise for you." Sirus said "I loved our date last night. I can't wait to see you again." Lilly typed back to Drake. "What if my dad catches me at your office?" She typed to Sirus. "I'm so glad I met you."

Drake texted back "He moved everything to his office at school because he doesn't want us together but I won't let anyone come between us." Lilly texted back. "Ok I can't wait to see you." Sirus texted her. "Xoxo."

Lilly began getting ready to go dress shopping with Rose. Prom was tomorrow. She put on her white dress that had daisies on it and some white dress shoes. She let her hair down to her shoulders. She put on some pink lipgloss.

She left her room and locked her door. Rose ran up and hugged her. "Ready to go?" "Yes!" Said Lilly excitedly. Sirus walked up and hugged her. "Sirus we got to be careful. What if someone sees?" "It's just a quick one since you are going to be gone almost all day." Said Sirus. "What are you going to do today?" "I got to help set up for prom tomorrow. I'll be thinking about you though." "I'll be thinking about you too. See you later." She said. "See you beautiful." He said as he walked away.

"So that's who you like. Who gave you the necklace though?" It's complicated but I started seeing my dad's boss first. Then I started falling for Sirus and I haven't told my dad's boss yet. I'm going to break it to him carefully." "Sounds complicated. I'm happy if you are happy though." "Thank you Rose. Off to the mall!"

They made it to the portals. Rose chanted "Mythics Mall". Soon they were there. They went to find some dresses. They were walking around and Lilly spotted a sparkling blue dress. "This is so pretty." Suddenly someone came up from behind her and put their arms around her waist. "Lilly behind you." She said as they both jumped.

She turned around to see Drake standing there. He wraps his arms around her and gave her a kiss on her lips. "Wow you taste yummy." Lilly blushed. "Rose this is my dad's boss and my boyfriend." "Drake this is my best friend Rose." "It's nice to meet you." "You too." Rose answered nervously. "What are you doing at the mall my princess?" "Shopping for prom dresses. I'm going with Rose to prom. What are you doing here?" "Well I was going to surprise you with gifts on our date tonight but since you are here you two can pick out whatever you want. I'll get you lunch too." Said Drake. "Really? You don't have to." She said hugging him. He kissed her again. "Id do anything for you." He said holding her hand.

She smiled at him but felt guilty because she loved both him and Sirus. "I really like this blue dress." We will get it then. You too pick out whatever you want." Said Drake. Rose picked out a red dress and some black dress shoes. Lilly grabbed sweet perfume and sparkly blue shoes to match her dress. They went to the checkout and it came to 300 dollars. She looked at Drake. He kissed her on the cheek reassuring her that it was ok.

"Thank you Drake." said Rose "No problem, a friend of my sweet girl is a friend of mine." "Can we get pizza for lunch please?" Asked Lilly as she batted her eyes at him. "Anything for you." The walked over to the food court and ordered pepperoni pizza and got some Pepsi. Soon it was ready. Drake grabbed the pizza and brought it to the table. He sat next to Lilly and kissed her cheek. She kissed him back. He grabbed a slice of pizza and held it up to her mouth. She took a bite and they smiled at eachother. "You guys look cute together." "Thank you Rose." Said Drake.

They continued eating and stealing kisses in between bites. "Thank you for a wonderful day. I got to get back to school though." She said hugging and kissing him. "I'll see you tonight." He replied giving her a kiss.

He teleported back his office. "Drake and Sirus both like you alot." "Ya I know. I don't want to hurt either of them. When we get back I want to put my clothes away then it will be dinner in a few hours." "Ya I want to do the do the same and try on my new dress!" Said Rose.

Soon they reached the portals. Lilly chanted "Magic Academy" and they appeared at the school's entrance. Lilly got to her room. "See you later Rose." "See you." She replied. She was about to shut her door when Sirus walked up behind her. He went in her room and Lilly shut the door and locked it before anyone could see. "I missed you!" She said hugging him and kissing him. "I missed you too. I see you picked out a pretty dress. I wish I could be your prom date." "Me too, maybe they will do a teacher student dance though and you can at least dance next to me." Said Lilly. "I'd love that!" Said Sirus as he kissed her again. "Tonight I've got to go shopping after dinner. Maybe I'll get something for my special girl." "You make me so happy." Said Lilly.

"I can't imagine my life without you." "I can't either." She said holding him tight. "I gotta go but I'll see you later." He said teleporting to his office.

Lilly put her dress away and sprayed some perfume on her neck. How was she going to choose between Drake and Sirus. She read quietly on her bed until it was time for dinner. She left her room and locked the door behind her.

Alan walked up to her and gave her a hug. "How was shopping?" "It was good but I ran into Drake and he insisted on buying me things and buying lunch. He was kind to me. I know that I need to distance myself though." "Yes Lilly you must be careful he is very dangerous." "I know dad, don't worry though I'm in love with Sirus." "You are? I'm glad. Let's get dinner before we are late. They got to the dining hall and she sat down. Sirus was smiling at her. She smiled back.

"This afternoon was interesting. Drake seems nice but I thought you liked Sirus." "I dated Drake first then fell in love with Sirus. I haven't found a way to break it to Drake yet." Replied Lilly. "Whatever you decide I'm here for you." "Thank you Rose." She said hugging her. It was grilled cheese and tomato soup for dinner tonight. They started eating and Lilly finished kind of quick. "Wow you were hungry." "I kind of have to leave for a date." Replied Lilly. "Oh I see. I hope you have fun. I'll see you tomorrow." She said hugging her. "Bye Rose."

Lilly started walking back to her room to change for her date. Sirus walked up behind her and Lilly quickly looked around to make sure no one was looking and pulled him into the room. He locked the door and held her close. They kissed eachother deeply. "I can't stay long because I need to get to the store before it closes but I just wanted to see you again." "I can't wait till I graduate so we don't have to hide." Said Lilly. "Me too, but it isn't long now." He said running his fingers through her hair. "I'll let you get some rest but I'll see you tomorrow." He said kissing her once more. "See you tomorrow." Said Lilly. Then Sirus teleported.

She felt guilty going to see Drake but she didn't know what else to do. She still had a little time before she needed to leave so she decided to try to relax and paint her nails a cute shade of pink.

Sirus and Drake were both at the same jewelry shop. Shopping for a ring for Lilly. "Getting a ring for your girlfriend?" He asked Sirus. "Yes, I'm hoping she says I do." "I'm doing the same." Sirus knows about Drake but not what he looked like. "I like this sterling silver ring with a small diamond. How much is it?" He asked the sales person. "1000 sir." "1000? Do you take payments?" Asked Sirus. "Yes if you can show proof of employment." "I work for the school I'm a professor.' He said showing his id. "Ok that's perfect you can split it and pay 200 a month for 5 months." "Thank you here is my payment." Said Sirus handing over his gold coins. "Here is your ring." Replied the salesmen. "I'll take this pink diamond ring." Said Drake. 'That will be 10000." "No problem here you are." He replied. "Thank you Mr Drake." He replied handing him the ring. Sirus now realized that he's Alan's boss. The one that's after Lilly. He quickly left to get ahold of Alan.

Drake teleported back to his office. Lilly was on the elevator on her way up to see him. Drake met her as she was getting off the elevator. He hugged her and gave her a kiss. "I got a surprise for you, follow me." He said taking her by the hand. They walked down the hall and went into a room with a private theater. "Wow this is so cool." "Glad you like it baby. We can cuddle and watch a movie. I have my own popcorn machine. There is also a candy and drink bar. " He said pointing to a big selection of candy bars, m and m's and more.

She ran over to it and grabbed some popcorn and peanut butter m and m's. "I already poured us some sweet wine. If that's ok with you." He said handing her a glass. She smiled and they walked down to the front row and sat down together. He flipped through the movies while she nibbled on her popcorn.

Back at the school Sirus caught up with Alan. "I was just at the ring shop picking up something for Lilly and Drake was there buying her a ring too. What's going on?" He said getting upset. "She was seeing him first because he pursued her but she told me last night that she is in love with you. I told her since he's dangerous she needs to distance herself slowly so he doesn't hurt her. So she's been seeing him less until one day she is going to break it off." "She loves me? He said excitedly. "I love her too. I bought her an engagement ring." He said showing Alan. "Wow, she is going to love that ring. I'm going to train her to defend herself against him just in case anything happens. " "I'll train her too. No one will hurt her on my watch." Said Sirus. "Thank you for taking care of my daughter." "I would do anything for her." Said Sirus.

Lilly and Drake were enjoying a romance movie together.

Sipping wine and sharing popcorn. She snuggled into his chest. She felt guilty but she loved both of them. The wine made her drowsy and she fell asleep into his arms. He smiled and kissed her forehead. He knew she had to be home soon but didn't want to wake her. He teleported her back to her bedroom and placed her on her bed. He covered her up and wrote a note and placed it by her bedside. It said

"You fell asleep so I brought you home. Thank you for a wonderful night. I love you." He teleported out.

Chapter 5: Prom Night

Lilly thought alot about Drake's note. She has not even told Sirus that she loves him. Truth is she loves them both. She texted him "Thank you for last night. I love you too." She started getting ready for today. She was excited for prom last night. The next day was her birthday. There was a knock on her door. It was Sirus. She pulled him in and locked her door. They kissed passionately while he held her in his arms. "I have a surprise for you later today during your free period. Just meet me in your dad's office okay?" "That sounds wonderful, I can't wait." She replied, kissing him again.

"Lilly I've been working up the courage to say this but I think I'm finally ready. I love you." Her eyes lit up and she jumped in his arms. "I love you too!" She said as she kissed him. "I can't wait to show you your surprise later. I better get going." He set her down and kissed her again. "See you soon my love." "See you baby." She replied as he teleported away.

She's in love with two people. Unsure of what to do but her heart feels full and happy. All she could think about was both of them. She decided to go to her dad's office instead of class to ask for advice. She let professor Emma know she wasn't feeling well and she excused her from class. "Hey dad can I talk to you for a little" "Sure princess what's the matter?" She stepped in his office and closed the door.

"Drake and Sirus both confessed their love for me and I told them I loved them." "Do you love them equally?" "Yes." She replied with a sigh. "Do you know that Drake has killed people in the past?" Lilly stepped back in shock. "He has?" "Yes, a lot of people that have gone against him have ended up dead. I have kept my loyalty to him for that reason. So no harm comes to either of us." "He is always so kind to me though." "He will be until you turn him away. That's why we must train, so you are ready when that day happens." "What if he just lets me go?" "I highly doubt he will. Try not to worry though. Sirus and I will defend you with everything we have. We love you." He said hugging her and kissing her cheek.

"I love you too dad." She said kissing him back. "Tomorrow is your big day. Your teachers already know so just stop by my office after you wake up ok." "Ok dad I got to get to my boyfriends class. I love you." "I love how your eyes light up when you talk about Sirus. You two are meant to me. " "I know dad I just don't want to hurt Drake. I know what you said about him but I really love them both." She said getting teary eyed. He pulled her into a hug. "I know sweetie don't cry. We will figure it all out." He kissed her forehead. "Ok dad i really got to go." They waved goodbye.

She soon got to Spell class. She got there early to see Sirus. He smiled big, pulled her into his arms and kissed her. Then he stopped so no one would see. "I missed you my love." "I missed you too." She replied smiling. "Don't forget after my class go to your dad's office but let me get there first. So I can give you a surprise." "It's not a surprise if you tell me." She giggled. He giggled back. Soon the students started coming in. Rose sat next to Lilly. "I see you blushing. Were you two kissing before class?" "Maybe." Lilly said, smiling.

"Alright today we will be practicing somewhat productive spells. I've created a mess on one side of the room. You will be learning how to tidy up just by the wave of your wands. Lilly why don't you show them how it's done." Lilly got up and concentrated on cleaning up. She waved her wand and caused a broom and dustpan to start picking up the broken pieces on their own and collecting the dirt. "Well done." "Everyone else why don't you give it a go?" The students started waving their wands and soon the messy room was cleaning itself. "See, I knew you all could do it. That's all for today class dismissed." Said Sirus. "Ok I'm headed to the office take your time ok." He said winking at her.

"Sirus has a surprise for me so I have to take my time." She said smiling at Rose. "You will have to tell me what happens." She said excitedly as they stood in the hallway. "I will, are you excited for prom tonight? "Yes I am." "Me too I just wish I could dance with Sirus." "That would be cute." She replied. "Ok I cant wait anymore I hope he's ready for me.* "Good luck." Said Ross as she hugged her. Lilly walked slowly to her dad's office. She walked in and shut the door. The lights were off. Suddenly they came on and the whole room was covered in beautiful pink flowers. Sirius was dressed in a handsome black suit and her dad was standing by with his phone camera on.

Sirius approached her and got on one knee. "Lilly, ever since you came into my life I knew you were my soulmate. Will you marry me?" He said opening a small box revealing a pretty ring. Lilly started crying but she was smiling. "Yes I will!" He slipped the ring on her finger and pulled her into a kiss. Alan filmed the whole thing and got a few photos. Lilly kept crying tears of joy as Sirius held her.

Her dad came over to hug Sirus. "I trust you to keep my daughter safe." "I will sir, I'd give my life for her." Lilly knew at this moment that she needed to end things with Drake soon. Sirius was the one for her. He kissed her again.

"I'm so happy for you both and I hate to cut this short but we need to go before we are caught in here. As soon as you graduate though , you both can kiss in public all you want." "I love you baby." She said kissing him one last time. "I love you too. Take some of these flowers for your room. I'll see you later my love. " He said, handing her the flowers and then leaving the office.

"I'm so happy dad but on the other hand I'm really scared. I'm going to have to end things with Drake soon." "Don't worry we will protect you. It's almost time for dinner and then prom." "I know dad I'm so excited for prom. I'll try to keep my mind off things. I love you." She said hugging him. "I love you too princess." She left to go to her room for a short break before dinner. She got to her room and shut the door.

Drake starts calling her. Her heart sank. She wasn't going to tell him anything bad right now. "Hi baby how are you?" "I'm doing well my beautiful lady. Happy almost birthday. I have a surprise for you tomorrow morning but I won't keep you out of school long. Meet me at my office. In fact I'll teleport you there so you don't get caught." "Ok I can't wait." "I love you." "Love you too." She replied. They hung up together.

She starts feeling worried. What if he proposes. She will have to say yes or else. She tries not to think about it. She decides to head to dinner early. Hoping to see Sirus. She says down next to Rose who is reading a book. "I have an announcement for you all." Said headmaster Morse getting everyone's attention. " We have a professor here that will be staying with us till the end of the school year. He is here to seek out exceptional students for their advanced magic program. I've already given him the phone numbers of the students with the highest grades. He will be reaching out to you all shortly to talk to you about this opportunity. So let's give a warm welcome to professor James." The students clapped. Professor James was handsome with shoulder length black hair and green eyes.

Suddenly Lilly got a text. "Hi Lilly this is Professor James. It's a pleasure to meet you. I look forward to speaking with you sometime." Lilly showed the text to Rose. "Oh looks like Sirus has competition." She said teasingly. "Nope, because guess why? She said excitedly as she showed Rose the ring. "He proposed?" She asked a little too loudly. Sirius looked over at them and smiled. Lilly smiled back."Yes and I said yes!" They hugged eachother. "I'm so happy for you!" "Thank you!" She replied.

Dinner came but they didn't eat much. Don't want to dance at prom on a full stomach. "I brought my dress with me. I figured we could get ready in your room." "That's a great idea." Said Lilly. They walked to her room and suddenly Sirus came up to them. Lilly pulled them in the room and locked the door. Sirus pulled her into a kiss. "We gotta be quick the dance starts soon. " "I know, sorry for interrupting. I just wanted to see my fiance." "You both are so cute." Said Rose. "Don't worry i can leave before you get changed. " "Well you can watch me change." Said Lilly as she down to her bra and panties. "Wow you are so beautiful." "I won't touch though. That is for marriage." "A true gentleman." She said pulling him into a kiss. "I'll leave so we can all get ready. I love you." "Love you too." She replied. He teleported to his office.

Rose got undressed to get her dress on as well. "You two are a perfect match but Drake seems to love you too." "I know but I will be leaving Drake. It's for the best." They continued getting ready. They straightened each others hair and put lipgloss on. Soon they were ready.

They walked down to the school auditorium to see all the chairs gone and everything transformed into a dance hall. The teachers were lined up on the walk to chaperone the kids. There were cool decorations and even a DJ and a snack table. Sirus was smiling at Lilly but Professor James was looking at her too which felt a bit odd.

Lilly and Rose went over to grab a cookie and some soda. Then they sat down over by the teachers since no one was dancing yet. Sirus walked over to them. "You look so beautiful." He whispered to Lilly. "Be careful baby I don't want to get you in trouble but you are so handsome." "Thank you I love you." "Love you too." She replied as he walked away. The new professor suddenly walked over to Lilly. Sirus eyed him as he did so. "Lilly, it's a pleasure to meet you." "How do you know I'm Lilly?" She questioned. "The headmaster pointed out all the A+ students to me." He lied. "Oh ok nice to meet you." He shook her hand. "Likewise. I hope I can see you in my office for a few minutes tomorrow morning to discuss putting you in an advanced program when you graduate." "Id love to but tomorrow is birthday so it will have to be quick." "I completely understand. I'll text you tomorrow." "Ok." She saw Sirus staring daggers at him. She pulled out her phone to text him.

"Don't worry baby he was just talking to me about the magic program. I love you so much my future husband." Sirus got the text instantly and said "I figured baby but I don't want anyone taking me from you. I love you." She got the text and smiled back. Winking at him.

Soon the music started and the kids got on the dance floor. Sirus noticed that new professor looking at Lilly again. "Why do you keep staring at Lilly?" He asked. "I'm not I'm looking at everyone." He replied. Alan pulled Sirus aside and whispered to him. "Be careful we don't know who this guy is . For all we know might be a spy for Drake. If Drake's find out about you before we are ready." I understand, I'll be careful." Replied Sirus. The girls continued to dance. A few songs went by and then the DJ announced that the teachers could dance now.

Sirus danced next to Lilly but tried to be nonchalant about it. Professor James watched them but they tried to not pay attention to him. Lilly and Sirus keep smiling at eachother. He whispered in her ear "I can't wait till we are dancing at our wedding." Lilly blushed. "I can't wait either." They continued dancing and soon Prom was over. Lilly headed to her room and locked her door. She was so tired that she slipped into her PJs and headed to bed.

CHAPTER 6 WILL YOU marry me?

LILLY WOKE UP TO HER phone ringing it was Sirus. "Happy birthday my beautiful fiance!" He said excitedly. She yawned. "Thank you baby." "I'm sorry for waking you. When you are ready come to your dad's office ok. I love you." "I will honey I just need to get ready and shower. Love you too." She hung up. Just got a text from professor

James. "Happy birthday. Can you meet me later on to go over the program?" "Yes I can and thank you I'll text you later." Just then Drake called her. "Happy birthday my love are you ready to come over? "Hi baby I'm still in my pj's. "That doesn't matter it will just be us." "Ok teleport me over. I can't stay long though because my dad and Rose are expecting me." "This won't take long my love." With that she was in his office in an instant.

"Wow that was fast" she said. He pulled her into a kiss. "You look cute in your pj's but don't worry you won't be in them for long. His whole table was filled with gifts wrapped in pink paper. "Are all these for me?" "Yes my love and that's not all." He suddenly teleported Alan there. "Why am I here, what's going on?" He asked looking at them. "I know you hate me and think I'm a monster but I promise to treat your daughter well. He got down on one knee. "Lilly will you marry me?" He said showing her the pink diamond ring. She looked up at her dad scared at how to answer. He mouthed just say yes. "Yes." She replied. He slipped it on her finger. Luckily Sirius's ring was on her nightstand.

Alan must choose his words carefully but first he texted Sirius. "Running late I'm sorry but see you soon." "Please don't hurt my daughter." He begged. Drake pulled her into his arms held her tight. "This is my future wife, my queen. I will never hurt her." He said sincerely. "Drake I'm trusting you." Said Alan extending his hand towards him. Drake shook it. "You have my word. I will even drink a truth potion." "I might take you up on that." "Lilly open your gifts so you can get back to school. She started opening them quickly. First was a beautiful jewelry box with roses painted on it. "Wow I love it " Second was a sunflower dress. Drake snapped his fingers and she was out of her PJs and into the dress. "Wow this is beautiful." She said kissing him. The rest of the gifts were exquisite jewelry. Including a pink diamond bracelet and another gorgeous necklace. She hugged him and kissed him. "Thank you for everything. I love you." They kissed once more. "I love you too baby. I will see you later. Thank you Alan for letting me be with your daughter. Whenever you want I will drink that potion. Goodbye my love." He said teleporting them back.

Lilly quickly put the ring and the jewelry away and put Sirius's ring on. "Im in shock I don't know what we are going to do." "I don't know dad but he seemed sincere. I feel bad because I'm cheating on him." "Don't beat yourself up. He could be lying and we will find out soon. Let's get to my office. I love you." "Love you too dad."

They got to Alan's office. Sirus and Rose jumped out and yelled "surprise!" Lilly jumped up and down. She hugged Rose and kissed Sirus. "Happy birthday my beautiful fiance." He said kissing her. He handed her a pretty wrapped box. Lilly opened it. It was a lovely butterfly bracelet. "I love it baby thank you." She says putting it on right away. Rose handed her a box too. Lilly opened it. It was a heart necklace with their picture on it that said bff's forever. "Aw thank you." She said hugging her. Her dad handed her something too. She opened it up. It was a photo album of pictures of her growing up. It said on the front "To the best daughter in the world I love you." She got teary eyed and hugged him. "I love you so much dad." "I love you too princess."

"Soon you will be graduating. Then we don't have to hide our relationship. I can't wait." He said pulling her in for a kiss. "I can't wait." She replied kissing him back. "I unfortunately have to go teach but we can see eachother later ok baby. I love you." "I love you too." She said kissing him. Sirus walked back to his classroom. "I'm glad you are having a good birthday honey." "Thank you dad."

Suddenly Professor James walked in the office. "Hi I'm sorry to interrupt but I was wondering if I could steal Lilly for a minute." "I'll see you later dad." She said hugging him. "See you princess." "Bye Rose." "See you Lilly." Professor James began walking her to his office. Once they got there he shut and locked the door.

"It's a pleasure to have you alone Lilly." He said kissing her hand. "Why did you lock the door?" She asked nervously. "I just didn't want anyone listening in." "Why it's just about the program isn't it?" "Have a seat please." She sat on a chair in front of his desk. He reached his hand across the desk and caressed her fingers. "I'm flattered and you are handsome but I'm engaged." she said. "I know you are. How's Drake doing?" She took her hand back. "How did you know that?" "I'm not a Professor, I'm Drake's boss." "Why are you flirting with me then?" "I can do what I want and I want you." "I love him and I won't hurt him." "You are cheating on him with Sirus." She stayed silent. Afraid of what to answer.

"I'll keep it a secret if you see me as well. I've killed a lot more then Drake so I suggest you don't refuse me. Maybe you will like me more then them." Lilly started crying. He wiped her tears. Then he kissed her on the cheek. "Dont mention this to anyone or else." "Why me? I'm not special." "You are though. You just don't see it." Lilly stood up and he pulled her into a hug. "Please give me a chance." He kissed her on her head. She looked up at him still crying. He lifted her chin up and brought her lips to his. He kissed her gently. She felt drawn to him but scared of him. She kissed him back. Like he had a spell on her.

"That's my girl. I'll let you get on with your day." She left his office. She ran to her room and locked the door. She texted Drake and tried to tell him what happened but it was like some sort of force was holding her back from getting the words out. "Drake I ..... she managed to send. He sensed something was wrong and teleported her there. She frantically started crying and held onto him. She tried desperately to speak but she couldn't. "Sweetie calm down what's wrong?" She tried to speak again but couldn't.

"Jared did this to you. He must have infiltrated the school. You must do what he says for now till I figure out a plan. He is a alot stronger then me . He's a monster and will do anything to get what he wants. That's why you can't say what happened or type it. He has a hold on you that is preventing you from saying anything. I'm sorry for being with you. That's what drew him to you. Now you are in danger." She kept crying. "Please forgive me. I will let your dad know what's going on. I will let Sirus know too." "Yes I know, and I know your dad told you to be with him because I would hurt you. I forgive you and I love you. I just hope in the end that you keep me in your life." "I will I love you I'm sorry." She cried.

He held her tight. "I will always love you I promise. I'm not mad at you." She reached up and kissed him. He kissed her back passionately. "I know you got to get back to school before anyone suspects something but I know you are quite traumatized so I will teleport back with you." They got back to her room. He called Alan. "Alan I know you don't want to talk to me but it's important. Please come to Lilly's room now." Alan teleported there. "You can't be in the school and why is she crying?" Lilly held unto Drake. "It's Jared he's in the school. He's already cursed her. She can't tell me who he is because of it. He's likely in disguise. I also know about Sirus. Whatever she chooses I just want to be in her life."

"We need a plan to get rid of him. I'm trusting you that you are being sincere." "I am Alan, I need to go though before I'm caught. I love you Lilly." He said kissing her. "I love you too." He teleported away. She cried into her dad's arms. "I'll make sure he doesn't hurt you. I will let the school nurse know that you are sick so you can get out of your classes. I'll have Sirus come by later too. I love you." "Love you too dad." He left the room and walked to Sirus's office.

"Where Lilly?" Alan pulled him off to the side. "Drake's boss in the school and he put a curse on her. We are not sure how to break the curse. Drake also knows about you. He isn't angry he just wants what's best for her. Drake's boss silenced her so she can't speak his name or show who he is." "I bet it's Professor James. He's always staring at her." "We will have to find out. " "I'll do anything to protect your daughter." "I know you will."

Sirus walked with Alan to Lilly's room. She had finally stopped crying. "Hi sweetie it's me." Lilly opened the door and jumped into Sirus's arms. They walked into her room and closed the door. He kissed her deep. "Your dad told me what happened. I'm here for you and we think we know who did this to you. Professor James. Lilly tried to nod her head and speak but couldn't. "I knew it. I won't let him hurt you." Said Sirus. "I love you." "I love you too my sweet girl."

"You take it easy for tonight and rest in your room. I'll check on you later. I love you princess." "I love you too dad." "I'll be checking on you too my baby. " "Thank you honey." They both left the room.

Lilly laid down on her bed. Her phone went off. She really didn't have the energy to answer it but she felt a necessity to get up to check it. It was Jared. "Why am I not seeing your pretty face at dinner? "I don't feel well I'm laying down." "Well then I'll have to visit you in your room." Lilly tried to resist him even with the curse. "I really don't feel up to it. Can I see you tomorrow?" "No." He replied and then teleported to her room.

She sat up and started to cry. He sat on her bed and pulled her into a kiss. She kissed back like she couldn't help herself. Like her body depends on his touch to survive. That was part of the curse. Instead of trying to woo her like a normal person he made her need him. She felt better the more she kissed and held him. The curse had a drawback though. She needed him to feel better but he also needed her. They needed eachother to have happiness and strength

They continued to kiss until there was a knock on her door. He teleported away. It was Rose. She hugged her. "Your dad told me what happened I'm so sorry." "It's ok , I know everything will work out in the end. "Wow you seem so positive." It was Jared's affect on her. She was on a high because they were just kissing but soon she would crash. "I hope tomorrow is a normal day." "Me too." Said Lilly.

Chapter 7: Jared's Curse

She woke up the next morning feeling tired and sluggish. Jared texted her. "I need my baby. I'll be there soon." He suddenly teleported there. He held unto her and ran his fingers through her hair. "No." She said faintly. "You need me." He whispered in her ear. He began kissing her and she craved his touch more. She kissed him back and he eventually he started kissing her neck. This sent shivers down her spine. Drake started calling her. He picked up the phone. "I'm busy kissing your girl." "Drake help." She said but he kissed her to keep her quiet. "I will kill you." Hissed Drake. "Is that so?" Said Jared as he teleported to Drake's office.

"This is my women now. If you would have married her in time she would have been safe. Now it's too late. I think I might erase her memory so she never knew you." "Don't do that! I love her." He put his wand on Drake's neck. Lilly suddenly teleported there and hit Jared with a knock back spell. He fell to the ground. She stood in front of Drake. "You may have cursed me but I will never love you." "You may not get to make that choice. He drew his wand at the both and cast a paralyzing spell. They fell to the ground. He went over to Lilly and kissed her so Drake could see. "See you soon my girl." He teleported away. Drake's assistant heard everything and rushed in to help them. He waved his wand and soon they could move. Lilly began shaking and went into shock.

"I need to get her to the school so her dad can help her but I don't have my strength. " "I will help sir." He held onto both of them and they teleported to Alan's office. "What happened?" asked Alan. "It was Jared who attacked us. We need to get him out of the school." Said Drake. "I'll go tell the headmaster. You two can't be seen at the school." "I'm not leaving my fiance." Drake said sternly. Lilly leaned on him. She felt so weak. Alan met up with Sirus and Jared happened to be talking to the headmaster. "Morse, you need to ban that professor. He isn't a real professor. He is Jared, Drake's boss. "You are lying." Replied Jared.

"I'll investigate this but until I have proof I won't just kick him out." "He attacked my daughter!" Said Alan angrily. "You will talk to me with respect! I'm going to ban you from campus for the rest of the day. Tomorrow you may plead your case." "He did attack her!" Yelled Sirus. "Be careful or you will be gone too." Warned Morse. Jared must have cursed Morse to agree with him. He smirked at them as they walked away. Professor Emma was with Drake and Lilly. "I heard what happened and gave Lilly a healing potion. She is resting for now." "Thank you so much." Said Alan.

"Sirus I can't stay here to look after her so I'm trusting you." "I will guard her with my life. He kissed Lilly on the forehead. "I will find a way to save you. I love you." He then teleported.

"We will find a way to break this curse Alan." Said professor Emma. "Sirus please keep watch on her in her room and keep the door locked. I will place a protection spell so hopefully he can't teleport in." Said Alan. They walked to her room while Sirus carried her. "I'll work on some strength potions for her." "Thank you Emma. I love you my princess." Said Alan as he kissed her forehead. Sirus set her on her bed and locked the door. Alan placed a protection spell on the room.

Sirus covered her up and laid next to her. Holding her as she slept. He started crying. He wishes that Jared never met her. Suddenly her phone dinged. It said professor James. "I will have you soon my future bride. I won't let anyone stand in my way."

Sirus called Drake from Lilly's phone. "Lilly are you awake baby?" "No Drake it's me. Jared texted her she's still sleeping. It says he's going to make her marry him and will stop anyone in his way." "Alan and I are trying to figure out something just please protect her. " I will just please promise me one thing. Can I stay in her life even though she has you." "Of course Sirus. Talk you you soon."

He laid back down and held her tight. "I wish I had never met Lilly. Then she wouldn't have been in danger." "I work for you, he would have still found out about her. Don't beat yourself up. I know you care about her. I'm sorry for pushing her towards Sirus." "It's ok I know you were just looking out for her. Jared is more powerful than anyone though. He can control whoever he wants. Lilly keeps trying to fight him but I see how tired she's becoming." "We will find a way to save her. Once I get back to school tomorrow I will keep him away from her."

Chapter 8: Jared

SURPRISINGLY JARED left them alone last night. Lilly and Sirus started waking up. "Good morning my love. How are you feeling? "Tired." She replied as she kissed his lips. "Emma dropped off a few strength potions. Drink one it should help. Lilly drank one down. It tastes like berries. "Thank you baby." She replied kissing him. She got out of bed. "Can you help me get some clean clothes on? I just feel weak." she started taking her clothes off but she left her bra and underwear on. Suddenly

Drake teleported there. "I know I'm not supposed to be here but I had to check on you." There was an awkward silence between him and Sirus. "I was helping her get dressed she isn't feeling well." He said defensively. He went over and held her tight kissing her deeply. "We are a team now. We both are with Lilly. I won't get mad at you or jealous of you." Said Drake.

Sirus kissed her and slipped her dress on. Drake got her socks and shoes on. "I love you both and again I'm sorry for everything." "Don't be sorry. We love you too." Said Sirus. "Honey it's me can I come in?" It was Jared. "We got you sweetie. I'm not scared of him." Said Drake. They opened the door and held onto Lilly. They raised their wands at him and made him back up. Morse was headed for them.

"I told you that Sirus was dating a student." Said Jared. "Sirus you need to collect your things and leave. You are lucky that you don't go to jail." "Morse this isn't you. He's controlling you. "You are evil and are not allowed here. You need to leave too Drake." "Headmaster Professor

James isn't a professor he's the evil one." Chimed in Emma as she was walking down the hall. "I don't believe any of you." Said Morse.

"I admit it, I'm engaged to Lilly. Fire me all you want but I'm not leaving her side." "Me either." Said Drake. "Come here Lilly. You know I'm the one you want to be with." Said Jared. She was drawn to him because of the curse but she fought it. She defiantly kissed Sirus and then Drake. He waved his wand and pulled her out of their arms. Without hesitation Drake punched Jared in the face and he fell to the ground. His face bloody. Morse in return hit Drake with a paralization spell. Sirus then cast the same spell on Morse. He grabbed Lilly from Jared and ran with her. Emma healed Drake and left Morse. Then she chased after Sirus. Hoping to help somehow. Drake trailed behind. Still recovering from paralysis. Jared recovered quickly and teleported in front of Sirus. Stopping him in his tracks. Alan suddenly arrived at the school and they all stood by Lilly.

"I don't care how many people help you. You won't beat me." Sneered Jared. He cast a spell paralyzing all of them then he swooped up Lilly and teleported. One he teleported all the curses were lifted and everyone could move again. Morse had no knowledge of being cursed.

Jared destroyed the necklace around Lilly's neck so Drake couldn't track them. Then he cast a spell knocking her unconscious and erasing her memory. The curse however was lifted. He was going to try to get her to fall in love with him.

"I can't track her he must have destroyed the necklace I gave her." Said Drake crying. "We are going to get my daughter back." Said Alan.

Chapter 9: Welcome to your new home

Lilly is sleeping at an undisclosed location. No one knows where Jared lives and no one ever dared to ask. Apart from being kidnapped and her memory erased, she is doing ok. "I hope you like your new life." He said running his fingers through her hair. She started waking up and looked at him. She flinched at his touch. "Who are you? Where am I? "I'm your boyfriend, you are home my baby. "Why don't I remember anything? "You were in an accident and a witch erased your memory. I saved you."

"This doesn't feel right. Like I shouldn't be here." "You are just recovering from everything. Soon it will all feel normal." He leaned down to kiss her but she moved her head away. He stepped back frustrated. She was still drowsy and drifted back to sleep. He contemplated cursing her again but he wanted her to love him the correct way.

He set out to get her some flowers and chocolate. He's hoping that will help break the ice.

"I can't believe she's gone. My daughter is gone. What are we going to do?" Cried Alan. "We will figure out a way to find her." Said Sirus. "I'm going to kill him for taking her." Said Drake. "Attention students and staff, one of our own has been kidnapped by a dangerous criminal named Jared. If anyone wants to help us rescue Lilly please step forward." Said Morse. Emma and Rose and several others stepped forward. "I'm trusting in all of you. Let's get her back." Said Morse.

Lilly woke up and had to use the bathroom. Luckily there was one attached to the bedroom. She went pee and went to get back in bed when he walked in the room with the chocolates and roses. She started backing up towards the bed. "Please don't be scared of me." She sat on the bed. He handed her the gifts. "Thank you." She replied timidly. He touched her cheek. She tried not to flinch. He pulled her face up to his and kissed her lips. "There that wasn't so bad was it?" "I don't know." "Please don't treat me like this." "I can't help it I don't remember anything."

"I'll leave you alone then." He was getting angry. "You can stay if you want." "If you don't want me to kiss you or anything, and you are pushing me away what's the point" "I'm sorry." She said as covered up with the blanket and started crying. He laid down next to her in bed and held her. "it's ok."

He said trying to comfort her. "Can you just sit here with me?" "Can I at least cuddle you?" "Yes." She said figuring that he wasn't going to give up.

He laid next to her and held her tight he was regretting his plan already. She wasn't falling in love with him fast enough.

Chapter 10: Memories

A couple days went by and everyone at the school was still trying to figure out a plan to save Lilly. Jared wasn't having much luck winning her over and was getting impatient.

Lilly started putting on a dress that he got for her. It was pink with white roses. He suddenly walked in the room while she was slipping her shoes on and pulled her into a kiss. "Your lips taste amazing. You are wearing the strawberry lipgloss I got for you." He said smiling. "Thank you."

"I was hoping you would kiss me back or hold my hand." She reluctantly kissed him back. "Why don't you love me yet? We were madly in love before you lost your memory." He lied. "I don't know, I'm sorry." She said looking down. "It's ok I'll be right back." He said kissing her again. She sat back down on the bed. Some of her memories started coming back. "I was going to the magic academy and I don't know this man. I need to get out of here." She looked around and realized he had a teleporter in his room.

"The magic academy." She chanted. She was whisked back to the from of the school. Rose happened to be outside. "It's Lilly!" She yelled. Sirius, Alan and Drake came running to her. Alan scooped her up. "Who are all of you?" She asked. "Rose go get the memory potion from Emma." Said Alan. Professor Emma heard the yelling and was already on her way with the potion. "Lilly drink this it will help." She said holding it up to her lips. She drank and her memories started coming back. She started crying. "Get her in the school before he comes after her." Said Sirus.

They rushed in the school carrying her. They went into Sirus's office and locked the door. Casting protection spells on the door too. Lilly sat down on a chair, she was feeling weak. Sirus and Drake kissed her on her cheek and each held one of her hands. Emma gave her a healing potion. She drank it down. "We are so glad you are safe." Said Drake. "He could come back any minute to try to take her. If she got married though her bond would help fight him off. I know timing isn't ideal but we don't have a choice." Said Alan. "Both, I want to marry you both please." She begged. "Ok it's settled then. Please stand up and hold hands together." They stood up. She was still wobbly but ready. "Do you Lilly take Drake and Sirus to be your husbands?" "I do." She replied kissing them both. "Drake and Sirus do you take Lilly as your wife." "We do." They said in unison. "You may kiss eachother." Said Alan. They gave eachother kisses. The marriage was recorded in the record book.

"Jared has broken into the school." Said Morse as he rushed towards them. "Ok we are ready." Said Lilly. The drew their wands together and waited for him. He appeared in front of them and knocked Drake to the ground. "Your too late you jerk. I'm happily married now. You lost." Taunted Lilly. Jared waved his wand and knocked back everyone but Lilly. He grabbed her by the throat and forced her into a kiss. Then he slapped her so hard she fell to the ground. "You shouldn't have refused me." Drake and Sirus stood up and brought her back on her feet. Alan , Morse, Emma and Rose recovered as well.

"Lilly chose us , you are finished." Said Sirus. They held unto Lilly and hit Jared with a paralyzation spell. He fell to the ground. Lilly put her foot right in his chest to hold him down. Morse chanted a spell that will prevent Jared from ever coming near her again. Alan cast a binding spell fusing his arms and legs together. It wouldn't last forever though. Finally Drake and Sirus held their hands together and sent Jared into another dimension where he would be trapped for a while.

They all hugged Lilly. "Thank you for everything I love you." "We love you too my princess." Said Alan.

Chapter 11: Epilogue

Lilly went on to graduate with Rose. She also received top honors. Sirus had to come clean about marrying Lilly. Morse choose not to fire him and apologized for the way he acted while he was under Jared's Curse. Drake bought a mansion big enough for him, Alan, Lilly and Sirus. He even hired an artist to paint her room how she wanted. She decided on pink walls with white hearts. A big fluffy pink bed and an indoor swing. Her room has a view of their own private lake, where Lilly has been learning how to swim. Alan decorated his room all black and they still have been debating on how to decorate the room that they share together.

It's been a weird situation but they try not to get jealous over eachother. Right now they are enjoying some wine in front of the lake. The lovebirds are laying on a blanket cuddling together and Alan is enjoying watching the sunset.

"I couldn't imagine a life better then this. Thank you for being with me." "Thank you for loving us." Said Drake as he kissed her. "I love you." Said Sirus as he kissed her. "I love you both so much." she replied as snuggled closer to them. They both kissed her cheek and settled their eyes on the sunset.

STORY NUMBER 2: DARKNESS Falls

LILA HAD BEEN ABUSED for a number of years but was scared to leave. She could rarely see her friends and if she did they had to be female friends. She had already been in an abusive relationship before and was scared to start over again. Every day she walked on eggshells. Hoping for things to get better. One day she found a band she really liked called Darkness Falls. They were a dark wave/rock band. The singer had a public profile. They were not a big band yet so the account wasnt verified. So there wasn't a clear way of telling if she was messaging the singer or someone pretending but she took the chance and added him.

Chapter 1: Alexander

Lila got up that morning to her boyfriend screaming at her because she was not up yet doing the dishes or cleaning the house. She knew better then to sleep in but she was so exhausted from doing everything. She got out of bed went to the bathroom and started the dishes before he got the opportunity to scream at her again. She finished those and then threw the laundry in the washer. He had left for work already so she took the time to take a shower in peace.

She turned on the hot water but had to turn on some cold because her body aches so much. Whenever she would do something wrong he would hit her and leave bruises and sometimes scratches. Her body was in so much pain. She washed up quickly so she could get out and finish the chores. The sooner she finished, the sooner she could rest before he got home.

She got out and dried off. Then she took out the garbage and swept the floor. The laundry wasn't ready for the dryer yet so she sat down and got in Facebook. She had recently been listening to a band she really liked called Darkness Falls. She had won two VIP tickets. Her friend Sarah was going to be taking her. Her boyfriend didnt care because he was happy to have her away from him for the night so he could flirt with other women online while she was gone. Scrolling through she noticed a profile for the singer of the band. Alexander Filatov. She added him and he must of been online because he accepted right away.

Lila didn't have her profile as in a relationship because her boyfriend wanted girls to think he was single so he could flirt with them. So I'm public he pretended she didn't exist. He only used her and didn't love her, but she was too scared to leave. She typed to Alexander.

Thank you for adding me. I love your band. He typed back. I appreciate you liking our music. I hope I'm not to forward by saying you are beautiful. She blushed and typed back. Thank you, but I must ask how do I know it's really you? Your profile isn't verified. He typed back. Since we are not a big band we can't get verified yet. You will just have to trust me. She typed back. Ok I really hope it's you. You are really handsome by the way. He smiled and typed back. Thank you, are you coming to our show in a couple days? She typed Yes I have vip tickets. He typed, Great it's a date then see you soon. I hope you will stay in touch. He hopped offline. She closed Facebook and put the clothes in the dryer.

She was happy for the first time in awhile. She just hoped he was real and not a scammer using his picture. Soon the clothes were done and she started to put them away. Her boyfriend just opened the door. "Did you do all the housework? he barked at her. "Yes." She replied timidly. "Good you can leave me alone and stay away from me." She went into her room to lay down for the night. She had a message from Alexander. She looked to see if her boyfriend was paying attention. He was too busy watching some cam girl.

Alexander wrote Hey, how is your day going? She typed back. Not great my boyfriend is cheating on me as usual and treating me like garbage. He answered, Oh you have a boyfriend ☹ She quickly typed back. He abuses me. I want to get away but I have no where to go and I'm scared. He typed, I'm so sorry you are going through that. I wish I could help you. She answered, Meeting you will be wonderful. I hope it's actually you. He typed, It will be me, and I will cheer you up. Goodnight beautiful ☺ She replied, Goodnight ☺

Chapter 2: Girls Day

"I have the day off I'm going to see John. Make sure the house is the clean then do whatever you want." He said leaving and then slamming the door shut. The laundry was done from yesterday so she just had to sweep and do dishes. She quickly got done and showered. Then she got dressed in a pretty pink dress. She texted Sarah. I'm ready, can't wait to see you. Soon she was there to pick her up. Lila slipped on her slides and locked the door. It was a beautiful August day.

"Thank you for picking me up. It's been a bad week." They drove to her favorite restaurant. Dixie Chicken. "I'm sorry I'm here for you. " "Thank you Sarah." They soon got to the restaurant. "Table for two please." Said Sarah. The waitress seated them facing the window. "What would like to drink?" "A margarita would be great." "Ok I'll need your id." Lila handed her it. "Thank you, and for you?" "A diet Coke please." The waitress disappeared to the kitchen.

"So what's been going on?" "He's been more abusive than normal. He's also still cheating on me." "I'm so sorry, at least you can come hang with me and we have that concert coming up." "I know I can't wait! I've got to show you something." She showed the conversation between her and Alexander. "Wow is it really him?" "I don't know I hope so." Suddenly he started calling her on Facebook. She picked it up nervously. "Hi how are you?" "I'm doing ok how are you beautiful?" I'm ok I'm surprised you called. Where is your video" "I'm busy packing for tour. Plus I don't want to show you my face till I see you. I want you to be surprised." "Ok it better be you though when I see you." "It will be, I promise." "I gotta go, I just wanted to hear what you sounded like. Talk to you soon, beautiful." "Bye handsome." She replied.

"Wow he likes you. I can tell you like him. Wouldn't it be amazing if he rescues you from that jerk you are with." "Ya but I just hope it's him not a scammer." The waitress came back with their drinks. "I'd like to order the chicken tenders and fries." "I'll have the chicken sandwich and and onion rings." Said Sarah. The waitress walked back into the kitchen. "I know you won't be able to leave looking pretty that day so I'll pick you up early and we can get ready at my house." "Thank you I love you." "Love you too." Replied Sarah.

Alexander texted What kind of flowers and candy do you like? She replied, Any kind of pink flowers and I love chocolate truffles. He replied Ok cutie see you soon ◈ She typed back ◈

"He said he's going to buy me flowers and chocolates." "Wow he sounds like a sweetheart." "Like i've said alot before. I hope it's not a scammer. Seems too good to be true that a rockstar would be interested in me." "Why not you are smart, cute and sweet." "Thank you Sarah. I'm glad you are my best friend." Soon their food came. "Wow this chicken is so juicy." "It's definitely the best chicken around." Said Sarah.

She sipped her margarita. "Mmm best drinks too." Lila giggled. They finished their food and left a small tip when the check came. "I can't wait till we go to the concert!" "Me either." Said Sarah. "I really don't want to go home and face him though." "I know but hopefully Alexander is your way out." "I hope so." She brought her home and unfortunately her boyfriend was already home. She hugged Sarah and cautiously went inside.

"Finally you are home. You need to make my dinner. I don't feel like making it. Make me a ham sandwich." She went to the kitchen to make him a sandwich. She brought it out to him with a bag of chips and a Pepsi. He didn't even say thank you. She went into the bedroom. "You arent going to eat you fat turd." He said. "No I ate with Sarah." She laid down in bed. She typed I can't wait to meet you tomorrow. He typed back. I can't wait either. Will you let me hold your hand? She started blushing. She typed back. Maybe but I hope you are real. I'm going to bed soon. He answered quickly. I am a real sweetie. See you tomorrow.

Chapter 3: Concert Day

Lila woke up and her jerk boyfriend was in the shower. She decided to start cleaning before he got the chance to yell at her. She got the beds made. They slept in separate beds. She also vacuumed. He got out of the bathroom. "Your concert is tonight isn't it?"He asked. "Yes." She replied quietly. "Can you stay the night at Sarah's? I don't want you waking me up when you come back." "Sure." "I'm leaving for work now. Get everything done before you leave." He said sternly as he left.

He texted a woman on his phone on the way to his car. The ball and chain is with her ugly friend tonight. You can come over for some fun.

Alexander messaged her. See you soon, beautiful. She answered back, Can't wait.

She finished cleaning and got dressed to meet Sarah. She didn't do it herself just in case he came back early. Soon she heard a honk. Sarah was there. She excitedly ran to the car with a change of clothes and some makeup. "He told me I could stay at your house tonight. I think he may be cheating on me but I'm happy to be away from him for the night." "Maybe you can spend the night with him." She said winking. "Ya in my dreams." "Let's get to my house so you can get changed and I can straighten your hair." They soon arrived at her place. She lived in a cute apartment with her cat named Mario.

"Hi kitty kitty." She said petting him. "He loves you." Sarah replied. "I want a cat but the jerk won't let me have one." "Let's get you ready." "Ok let me change in the bathroom and then you can fix me. I really appreciate this." "Anything for my bff." She changed into a pink dress and stepped out of the bathroom. Sarah grabbed the straightener and worked on her hair. "I can't wait to meet him. I hope it isn't a catfish." "I don't think he would go through all this effort if he were fake." Soon she finished and put some pink lip gloss on her. "You look so pretty." "You do too." Lila said.

"It's almost time. Let's go." Lila said. Sarah drives to the venue. It was small and held about 300. They hit up to the bouncer and showed him their passes. He walked them to the VIP room where the band was signing autographs. She stood in line with Sarah nervously. Finally it was their turn last. "Lila?" Alexander asked. She blushed. "Yes it is." She replied shyly but excitedly. "I told you it was me." He said smiling. "Let me finish up with the rest of the fans then I was to see you in private ok?" He said winking. She smiled and they stepped off to the side. "I can't believe it's him." She said. "I'm so happy for you. When he takes you to the room I'll just wait out here." "You can come in. You are my best friend."

They waited while he finished up. Then he walked over to them. "May I take you to my dressing room?" "Ok." "Your friend can come too." They followed him to the dressing room and he shut the door. He grabbed some flowers and chocolates that he had on his vanity. "These are for you." "Thank you so much." She said hugging him. "May we sit on the couch?" He asked. They sat on the couch with Lila in the middle. "Can I hold your hand?" He asked. "Yes." He put his fingers in-between her fingers. She started blushing. "So why are you interested in me?" "When I saw your picture online something about you intrigued me. I'm sorry you are going through an abusive relationship. I hope I can be the one to give you a better life." "You know, Lila doesn't have to be back until tomorrow." "Sarah, " she said, elbowing her. "Oh really? I got a hotel room with two beds." "Ok." She said shyly. He smiled and kissed her hand.

"The show is about to start. You both can watch from the stage if you want. I already told the band about you. They are happy for us. That is, they hope we will end up together." "After everything I've been through, I'd love a guy that will treat me well." "Well here I am." He said snuggling her. "Ok I gotta get out there. Let me walk you backstage. He held her hand and brought them up to the side of the stage. There were a few chairs set up. They both sat down. "I hope you enjoy the show sweetie." He gave her a kiss on the cheek. Then he walked on stage. "This seems like a dream. I really hope this isn't a dream." "It isn't a dream. Are you excited to spend the night with him?" "I'm so nervous." She replied.

"I want to dedicate this song to a special woman in my life. My girl Lila." He said for everyone to hear. Then he looked at her and blew her a kiss. She couldn't stop smiling. They started playing her favorite song. Rain dance. "This is the happiest I've been in years. I will never have a good day like this again. It's a fluke." She said, hanging her head. "What if you spend the night with him and never go home. You could be free and he wouldn't know where you went." "That sounds amazing." She said.

They finished that song and did a few more songs. She knew them all by heart. He made sure to keep looking her way and smie at her. She smiled back and felt so happy.

Soon the show was over. All the members started walking off the stage. He held out his hand and she took it. They both followed him to his dressing room. "That was an amazing show." Said Lila. "Thank you my love." "I hope you will take good care of my best friend." "I promise." He packed up his backpack. "Are you ready to head back to the hotel room? We need to take the tour bus there." "Why don't you sleep on the bus?" "We do sometimes but it gets cramped." "I'll see you later. I love you, please call me tomorrow." "I will love you too," said Lila.

They held hands and walked out to the tour bus. The rest of the band was already there. "Hi Lila, nice to meet you." said Zander the drummer. "How do you know my name?" "Alex has been talking about you non stop. He's in love." He said teasingly. "But she has a boyfriend." Said Alexander. "Not anymore I think I'm ready to walk away. I'm tired of being hit and screamed at." She said holding onto him. "Good you can travel with us. I'll get you new clothes and things. I'll protect you." "Thank you." She said crying.

"Sit down with me on the couch. Then once we get to the hotel we can settle in and order room service." She smiled and sat down with him on the couch. She laid her head on his shoulder and he wrapped his arms around her.

"I'm happy for you two. You have been looking for a good girl for a long time ever since your ex abused you." Said Benjie the bassist. "I'm so sorry you went through abuse too." Said Lila as she still was crying a little. "It's ok I'm just glad we found each other. "I hope you don't mind, I'm a little older than you." "I'm 30 and you are 45. Age is just a number." He smiled and kissed her on her head. Soon they arrived at the hotel. They all got out and went to the front desk. "Reservation for 5 under the name Alexander Filatov." "Very good sir, just sign here and take your room keys." "Thank you very much." He replied.

They walked up to their rooms. The two guitarists Benjie and Jordan shared a room together and Zander had a room to himself. Alexander and Lila went into their room together and locked the door.

The beds were covered in flower petals and there was a chilled bottle of champagne on the nightstand. He pulled her into a hug and kissed her cheek. "I know you've been through a lot so we can take things slow. I just want to make you happy." "I'm so glad I met you." She said snuggling into his chest. "I'm so glad too."

"Are you hungry?" "Yes please, can we order a pepperoni pizza?" "Yes we can. Why don't you sit on the bed and I'll order it now." "Ok." She went over to the bed and sat down. He grabbed the phone and called room service. "Hi, I'd like one pepperoni pizza please and a chocolate cake for dessert. Thank you."

"Ok it's on the way darling." He said sitting by her and putting his hand on her leg. "When we leave tomorrow I need to get a different phone. He's tracking this one and I don't want him coming after me." "We will get you a new phone tomorrow when we get to the next town

and we can go shopping. I'll have a little time before the next show."
"That sounds wonderful. Thank you for taking care of me." She said, kissing his cheek. "Anything for you my baby.

Soon there was a knock at the door. Their food has arrived. He tipped the hotel worker. There was a small table and chair set in their room. They sat down together. He popped the champagne and poured two glasses. "To our new lives together." He said as they clinked their glasses.

Chapter 4: Starting Over

He opened the pizza and gave her a slice on a plate. "Thank you, handsome." He winked at her. She bit into it. "Mmm so good." "I agree, I love pizza." He replied. "So where are we going tomorrow?" "Boston, we will be leaving sometime in the morning. Then once we get there you can get a new phone. Give your friend my number and take the SIM card out of your phone so he can't track you." "Ok I'll call her right now. "Hey Sarah I'm going to be getting a new phone so he can't track me. Alexander is going to send you his number till I get the phone. I'm going to travel with the band for now to get away. "Ok I love you, be careful." They hung up. Alexander texted his number to Sarah and she responded that she got it. Then Lila took the card out of her phone.

They finished their dinner and dug into the cake. "This is so sweet and delicious." "Not as sweet as you though." He replied. She started blushing again. They finished their cake and drank some more. They were both a little tipsy at that point.

"You want to cuddle and watch a movie?" That sounds great." She said happily. "I brought my pajamas with me in my purse. Let me get changed quickly." She went into the bathroom and got changed into a cute hello kitty shirt and pants set. While he got down to his t-shirt and a pair of shorts. "You look so cute." "So do you." She replied.

They got under the blankets together and he put his arm around her. "Do you think I'm doing a bad thing by just leaving and not telling him?" "You are doing the right thing. I had to do the same thing. My girlfriend did the same thing to me. She would hit me and threaten me but no one believed me." He lifted up his shirt and Lila noticed the scars on his stomach. She put her hand on them.

"I'm so sorry you went through that." She said lifting her shirt to show her bruises. He kissed her belly. "No one will hurt us ever again." He said. They smiled at each other and she snuggled closer to him. He started flipping through the channels to find a movie. Soon he found a comedy.

They started watching the movie together. Finally they both felt safe instead of scared. It wasn't long before they fell asleep in each other's arms. Soon it was morning. His alarm went off startling her. She jumped out of bed and thought she was going to get screamed at as usual because of her PTSD. He got up quickly and held her. She started crying. "It's ok you are here with me. No one will ever hurt you again. She started to calm down a little. He just held her there and kissed her forehead.

"I'm sorry, I'm just used to being hurt all the time. I think I'm just stuck in flight response." "It's ok sweetie soon you will be ok. I'm going to try to make you the happiest girl." "I'll try to make you happy too." She said looking into his eyes. He pulled her into a tender kiss that took her breath away. She started tearing up again. "I haven't been kissed like that in years." "He's a loser. You have me now." He said kissing her again.

Suddenly someone knocked on the door. "Who is it?" He asked. "It's Zander." "Come in." "How was your night lovebirds?" "Amazing." He replied. "Why is she crying?" "I kissed her and her loser boyfriend never treated her right." "Don't worry Alex loves kissing." "Stop it Zander." She blushed. "Everyone's ready so come down soon ok." "Ok."

"I gotta pee and get in my clothes." "Me too." He replied. So they both got ready separately and headed down to the tour bus. Meanwhile Mark, her loser boyfriend, was having a meltdown. "I can't track her. Where is that tramp? When I get my hands on her she's dead."

Lila and Alexander snuggled on the tour bus couch and they headed to Boston. They were currently in New York so they only had a few hours to go. Lila gave an update to Sarah and they talked for a little. Then they passed the time playing charades with the band.

Soon they arrived and pulled up to a Walmart. "Let's get some shopping done then we will head to the venue. I already booked a room for us. The guys are going to stay in the bus this time." "Ok baby, thank you again for being with me. I'm so lucky to have you." She said, kissing his lips. "I'm the lucky one." He said kissing her.

They got out of the tour bus and headed into the store. He wouldn't let go of her hand and that made her happy. Her loser ex wouldn't hold hands with her. They went over to the women's clothes. She grabbed a pack of underwear and socks. Then she found a couple dresses. "I have some band shirts you can wear too baby." He said as she pulled her into a kiss. "Ok baby." Suddenly someone took a picture of them. "Hey it's Alexander from Darkness Falls, I see you got a new girlfriend. I'm going to post this." "Go ahead I want the whole world to know that I found my soulmate." The paparazzi walked away.

"I guess you are getting famous." "Ya but all that matters to me is you." He said, smiling at her. They walked over to the phones. "Can I get this one for now?" She asked. She had picked out a 50 dollar prepaid phone. "Yes baby, that's fine. When we have some more money I'll get you a better one." "You don't have to do that." "Yes I do, you are my woman and you deserve the best." She started tearing up again because she hadn't had someone treat her so good before. "Ok we gotta check out so I can get ready for the show." They went and checked out.

"Thank you for everything. I'll pay you back when I can." "All you need to give me is your love." He said, kissing her cheek. The rest of the band were already back on the bus. "I got us all some snacks and sodas." Said Zander. He threw them some chips and handed them each a diet Coke. "Thank you." She replied.

She started nibbling on her chips while the bus started moving again. "You are cute when you eat." "Oh stop it." She said giggling. "Did you see the article online? Someone posted your picture." Said Benjie. "I know but I don't care. I love her." "You do?" She asked. "Yes honey, I loved you as soon as I saw you." "I love you too." She said kissing him.

"Mmm you taste like chips." He said as they both giggled. She finished her snack and snuggled into his chest. Soon they got to the venue.

Chapter 5: That's my woman

Mark was still angry not because he loved her but because he had no one to be his slave. He tried to convince his side piece but all she wanted was to sleep with him and not do anything else. An article popped up on his phone. "Darkness Falls lead singer Alexander gets a new lady" and there was a picture of him and Lila looking into each other's eyes. He got so angry he almost smashed his phone. "That little tramp! I'll show her!" He went and bought the cheapest ticket he could to the Boston show. The concert started in 3 hours and it would take two hours to get there. He got in his car and started driving as fast as he could.

Back at the venue the band was unloading their instruments and getting ready. Alexander and Lila were relaxing in his dressing room. He was putting on some black eyeliner and then some red lipstick. "You are so handsome." "You are so perfect." He replied. He brushed out his long black hair and put on a black leather outfit with studs. "You don't get hot in that?" She asked. "Yes, but I can always shower later." "One day maybe I'll shower with you." "That sounds sexy." He replied, winking at her.

They sat down and snuggled on the couch since they had time before the show. Soon people started arriving for the show including Mark. He got up to the guy scanning tickets and he held out his phone. "Ok sir you are in the standing only section which is right there." Mark went over there but when he wasn't looking, he went backstage. He saw a door with Alexander's name on it and kicked it in.

Lila grabbed onto Alex. "You are a tramp. How dare you cheat on me!" "We are over you abused me and cheated on me for years now." she shouted back at him. "Security!" Yelled Alex. "He stood up and got in Mark's face. "Get away from my woman you loser." Said Alex. Mark slapped him. Alex punched him back and he fell to the ground. The security guard came in and dragged Mark out. Alex's face stung from the slap. "I'm so sorry baby." Said Lila as she started to cry. "It's ok baby I'm ok. I'm sorry he came after you. Tomorrow we will file a restraining order." He held her tight. Zander came in the dressing room. "I heard yelling, are you guys ok?" "Ya we are fine. Her crazy ex came to stalk her." "You should have yelled for me I would have punched him." "Thank you my brother. I appreciate it. He said hugging him. Zander hugged Lila. ,"Your like our little sister now. If you need anything, you can call on any one of us ok." "Ok thank you." She said squeezing him back.

"Are you ok to go on tonight?" "Yes I am. Sweetie, are you going to be ok?" Yes baby I will. How much longer is the tour though. I'm hoping to move in with you and settle down soon." He got a big smile on his face and he kissed her passionately. "We have a couple more shows and then we can move into my house in Florida." "That sounds wonderful!" "Ok we gotta get on stage but I'll walk you to your seat on the side of the stage and you can watch me again." "Ok baby I love you." Love you too." They walked to the stage and she got comfy in her chair.

They went on and once again Alex gave a shout-out to Lila. Lila took the time to text Sarah and let her know that she missed her. She texted back that she missed her too. The crowd was energetic tonight. They even danced and sang along to the music. Alex once again would stop and blow her kisses. She kept watching him and smiling. She was finally starting to be at peace.

Soon the show was over and they both headed back to the dressing room. "That was an amazing show honey." She said, giving him a kiss. "Thanks beautiful, I can't wait for the tour to be over so we can settle in together. I'm paying off a duplex that's by the beach. The other band members live in the top half, we live in the bottom. We all moved in together so we could afford it." "That sounds good baby. I can't wait to wake up to you everyday." "Me either sweetie." He replied picking her up and hugging her tight.

Chapter 6: Moving In

The last few shows on the tour seemed to fly by. Soon they were packed up and headed home to Florida. "Thank you for being in my life." "Thank you for being in mine." He said pulling her close and kissing her. "What till you see the house. You will love it." Said Benjie. "Are you still going to get a restraining order?" Asked Jordan. "Probably not. I don't think he would follow me way out her. Plus Zander could just knock him out for me if he does show up." He flexed his muscles at them and smiled. Soon they pulled up to a nice white duplex that was right near the beach. They parked the tour bus in this massive garage and got out.

"Home sweet home baby." He said lifting her up. In his arms. Jordan unlocked the door and Alex carried Lila inside. "This place is amazing." She said looking around. A big TV, fancy kitchen, comfy couches. Alex walked her into the bedroom. There was a king bed and lots of blankets and fluffy pillows. She flopped on the bed smiling. He climbed on top of her and they started making out.

Zander placed an order for two large pepperoni pizzas and some wings. They stopped making out and walked into the kitchen. "I ordered some food it should be here soon." "Thanks brother." Said Alex. Lila looked in the fridge and saw some wine coolers. "May I have one?" She asked. "It's our house baby. You can just take what you want." He said giving her a big kiss.

Sarah started facetiming her. "Hi I missed you! I'm home let me show you the place." Lila walked around showing her the house, then she ran outside to show her the beach. The band followed her outside. Just watching her be so excited. "Wow I'm so happy for you. I love you." "Love you too. I'll talk to you soon ok." "Bye bestie." Said Sarah.

She ran back to Alexander and jumped in his arms kissing him. "I'm so glad I have you." "I'm so glad I have you too, my princess." Just as they were outside the pizza guy drive up. "That will be 50 dollars." Alex hands him 60. "Keep the change." "Thank you sir have a nice night."

They went inside and started devouring the pizza and wings. They all helped themselves to more wine coolers and we're soon tipsy and giggly. Lila started dancing with her pizza while one of their songs was playing in the background. Alex smiled and started dancing with her.

Once they were done with their food they all sat down to watch some TV together. Lila sat down next to Alex and they grabbed a blanket to cuddle under. The rest of the guys took the other couch. "Zander you are too big to be in the couch with us." Said Benjie. Zander was tall and very muscular. The other guys were kind of skinny and short.

"I didn't want to impose on the lovebirds." "It's ok I'll just bite you if you try anything with us." Said Alex giggling. Zander sat next to Lila. Lila hugged him. "See my brother I don't bite." He hugged her back and gave her a kiss on the cheek. She looked over to Alex and was shaking. She was a little worried that Zander might have just shown too much affection. Mark would always beat her if she even said hi to any men.

"Why do you look frightened babe?" He said holding her tight. Zander kissed my cheek. I thought you were going to flip out." "Baby we are family I don't care if they hug and kiss you on the cheek. Your lips are all mine though." He said kissing her deep. "Thank you for treating me good baby." "Thank you for not thinking I was a scammer." Said Alex.

They snuggled and continued watching TV. Soon Lila started yawning. "Do you want to go to bed my love?" "Yes baby." They got up and they all gave her hugs goodnight. Except for Zander , he was extra and gave her another kiss.

They went into the bedroom and locked the door. She slipped into her pajamas and he got into a tank top and boxers. They crawled into bed and covered up. "Why does Zander show me more affection then the others?" She asked quietly. "His wife passed away in a car accident a few years ago. He has not been ok since. You kind of look like her so I think that's why he's drawn to you. He understands that your mine but it's difficult because he still has that hole in his heart from when she passed." "Wow I'm so sorry he had to go through that. I don't want to get trouble or hurt your feelings though by showing him affection back." "I'm fine with you two holding hands, hugging or whatever because I know you won't go farther than that. He deserves to have someone that's comforting him. I can't ever see him having a girlfriend again because of what happened but I think you make him happy."

"Ok as long as you are sure it doesn't make you mad." "It won't baby because I know you will be marrying me and sleeping with me." He said winking at her. "Yes baby of course." She said, kissing him. They settled in for the night and put the TV on.

Chapter 7: Popping the Question

They had been dating for about six months and it had been amazing. Lila and Alexander still felt like they were living in a dream. They were so happy together. It seemed like a normal day. Lila and Zander were sitting on the couch together. Benjie and Jordan were out. "Baby I gotta go but I'll be right back. Stay here ok." "Ok baby I love you." They kissed. " Love you too." He left.

Her and Zander had gotten pretty close too. Alex knew about it though and was ok with it. Zander was her best friend. He slipped his hand in hers and kissed her cheek. She smiled and kissed him back. They loved holding hands but didn't do it much with Alex around because it felt weird.

Alex and his band mates were at the jewelry store picking out something for Lila. They were planning a big surprise for her. "I need to tell you something. I don't know if Alex told you already but I lost my wife in a car accident and you remind me of her. From your looks to your personality. It's almost like she had a long lost twin sister." "Alex told me the night I moved in. That's why he gave me permission to be close to you. He knows that I give you comfort and he wants you to be happy." He smiled wide at her and let out a sigh of relief. "I'm so glad you are ok with this. You do make a big difference in my life."

"When he first showed me your picture, I had started crying. I told him wow, you are so lucky. You found a girl that's a mirror image of my wife." "Wow." She replied tearing up. He wiped her tears. "Don't cry, I love you." Her eyes light up. "I love you too." He caressed her face. He kissed her on the lips so lovingly. She embraced it and kissed him back. "I'm sorry, I just had to know what it was like to kiss you. You are so much like her." It's ok but we can never do this again. Holding hands and cheek kisses are fine but I love Alex." "I know and I won't do it again I promise." "Thank you." She replied.

"I think this is the perfect ring for her." Said Alex holding up a beautiful diamond ring. "It's 1000 dollars." Said Jordan. "I'll finance it. She's worth it." He replied. "You still need to get some roses." Said Benjie. "I will do that." He paid for the ring and went to a flower shop next.

They continued to watch TV together like nothing happened. Soon the boys were back. "Hi baby I missed you." She said kissing him. "I missed you too princess." "Can you and the boys go outside for a little bit. I have something else I need to do." "Ok honey." Her and the boys went outside and sat in the beach chairs. It was nice and sunny out. You could smell the crisp water.

Alex got to work making a fancy Italian dinner for her. Yummy spaghetti, tasty sauce, buttered garlic bread. He even got a nice bottle of red wine. He hoped she would like it. He was even baking chocolate cupcakes for her with the sweet frosting she liked.

Outside Lila and Zander were sitting. They had their chairs next to each other and they were holding hands. "You are not worried Alex will get jealous?" Asked Benjie. "He knows we are best friends and that I promised not to be intimate with her. She also knows about my wife and she understands everything." "That's good." Said Jordan.

"Come in sweetie I'm ready for you." Called Alex. "We will stay out here for a little longer." Said Zander. "Ok love you." "Love you too Lila." She went in and Alex had candles set up along with a delicious dinner. "Wow baby this looks amazing." She said as he pulled her into his arms. "Anything for you my baby." They kissed and sat down to eat dinner. "This is the best dinner I've ever had." She said as she slurped a noodle. "You are so cute when you eat." He said giggling. She smiled back and dug into the bread. It was so warm and delicious. She sipped the wine. It was fruity. She soon finished and he handed her a cupcake. There was something sticking out of it. He came over to her chair and got on one knee. "You make me the happiest man alive. Will you marry me?" She pulled the ring out of the cupcake and started crying. "Yes I'll marry you." She licked the frosting off the ring and slipped it on her finger. Then she kissed him. "Mmm frosting." He said giggling. She started giggling. The rest of the band came in and turned the lights on.

"She said yes!" He excitedly kissed her again. "Benjie and Jordan congratulated her quickly, giving her hugs. Zander was a little bit slower because he wanted to be with her. He hugged her tight and kissed her on the cheek. "Alex is a lucky man to have you." He said, hanging his head. "I think I'll go to my room for a little bit." He said as he walked away.

"Did something happen while I was gone?" "Kind of but can we talk about it later? I just want to snuggle with you and eat some cupcakes." "Ok baby I'll bring some cupcakes into the living room." She sat down on the couch and covered up with a blanket. Jordan and Benjie sat on the other couch. Alex handed her a cupcake and wrapped his arms around her.

They watched TV for a couple hours and Zander still didn't come out of his room. "Can we go check on him babe?" "Yes princess." They walked to his room and knocked on the door. "Come in." "We got to tell you something." Said Zander. Lila went over and held his hand for support. "I kissed her on the lips. She reminds me so much of my wife that I had to kiss her. I'm sorry. Please forgive me." He said, tearing up.

"I know you really like her. I know how much she's like your wife. She's going to be my wife though. I can't picture my wife sleeping with another man. Holding hands and occasional cheek kisses is one thing but sex is too far." Lila started tearing up too as she squeezed both of their hands.

"I just can't believe you fell in love with someone who's just like her." He continued to cry. "I'm sorry that it happened that way. As soon as I saw her picture I was in love. She also went through the same abuse

I did." "I wish I could marry you both." She thought she said to herself but she accidentally said it out loud.

"What did you just say?" Asked Alex. "I didn't mean to say that out loud. I'm so sorry." He held onto him and started crying hard. "Shh it's ok sweetie. I know you love us both and it must be so difficult for you." "It's my fault. I shouldnt have been affectionate to you. Your his girl. That's my mistake." Said Zander. She went over and kissed his cheek. Her on face was soaked in tears. "I'm glad you both are in my life. I wouldn't change anything." He kissed her back on the cheek.

"Like I said before some kissing and handholding I'm ok with. No sex or making out though." "I know baby." "I still don't really know what to do though. This was supposed to be our happy engagement and you didn't tell me what happened right away. I am a little hurt." "I was afraid you would be mad.

That's why I didn't tell you." "I'm not mad, just upset. I think I need to be alone for the night. You can sleep on the couch or whatever." He said kissing her then leaving the room.

She grabbed one of Zander's pillows and cried into it. He reached over and rubbed her back. "This is my fault. I won't hold your hand or kiss you anymore. I don't want to break you guys up. She picked her head up and hugged him. "Did you really mean what you said about marrying us both?" "Yes I did. I feel like I'm supposed to be with both of you, but I can't lose Alex." "I understand, like I said I'll leave you alone." "Ok." She got up and left the room.

He filled in Jordan and Benjie on what happened. "She loves you dude. Don't let this ruin everything. You know how much she's been through and how much Zander's been through. They are probably hurting so much that her having both you and him probably is helping her healing process." Said Jordan. "Ya it's a lot of emotions for both of them." Said Benjie. Suddenly she walked into the living room and covered up on the couch. She was sobbing into the cushion.

He wanted to comfort her but instead they decided to go to their rooms to give her space. He laid in his bed. It felt empty without her. He started to cry. He didn't want to share her but couldn't risk losing her either. Seeing her cry broke his heart.

Chapter 8: Love is difficult

Zander got up that night to go to the bathroom. He went to check on Lila. He kissed her forehead and she started to wake up. "Alex?" She asked sleepily. "No it's Zander." "I love you Zander." She said reaching up to kiss his cheek. It was dark though so she missed and kissed his lips. This startled her because she ment to get his cheek. "I'm sorry I didn't mean to." She started to say but he took her lips in his and kissed her passionately. Alex suddenly walked up behind them. Scaring them both. Lila sat up shaking. "Don't hurt her please. It was me. It was dark and I went to check on her and she thought it was you. So she kissed me because she couldn't see who it was." He said in a panic.

Lila was in tears again. "I haven't decided what I want to do yet. I love my princess more then anything but I don't want you guys being intimate. Especially behind my back." "I won't baby I promise. I can't lose you." She said desperately. "I'm going back to bed. I love you but I need more time." He peed and went back to his bedroom. Zander was holding hands with her as she was still crying. "I know I already broke what I said about not kissing you but I guess I have to stick with it this time." "I love and I'm sorry for everything." Said Lila.

"Don't be sorry. You are the best thing to come into my life. Sometimes I just wish I met you instead of Alex." "I love you both though so that's what makes this hard. I wasn't expecting to fall in love with both of you. It just happened." He pulled her close and kissed her forehead. "Whatever Alex decides we will do. I can't lose him." "Ok honey we will see what he says in the morning. Why don't you get some rest." Said Zander. "I'm tired but I can't sleep. I'm so scared he will leave me because of this." She started to cry again. "He loves you more than he's ever loved anyone. He won't give up on you, trust me." she laid her head in his lap and covered up. He ran his fingers through her hair, trying to soothe her.

She fell asleep after a while and so did he. The rest of the band got up and came downstairs to check on them. Benjie pointed out that they were sleeping on the couch together. "It's ok I knew about it." Said Alex. He went over and sat next to Lila. He started rubbing her legs to wake her up. She got up scared and started apologizing. "We fell asleep, we didn't do anything, please don't be mad." Her heart was pounding so fast. Zander woke up and held her hand. "It's ok, I've got you." "Baby please stop being scared of me. I love you. I'm not your ex. I would never hurt you."

"I've thought a long time about all this. I know you love each other and I can't break my best friend's heart after everything he went through. But I also can't see my wife and my best friend sleeping together and making out. So this is what will happen. You both can still hold hands and kiss each other on the cheek. No making out though and try not to fall asleep together." "Thank you Alex!" She said jumping on him and kissing him. "I love you baby so much." "I love you too." She replied. Then she jumped to Zander and kissed his cheeks. She held him tight. He kissed her cheeks. "Thank you my brother for not kicking me out of your life. I love you both too much to lose you. I'm sorry again for kissing her the way I did." "I forgive you my brother."

"I'm going to make breakfast. You two may cuddle while I'm gone but once I'm back she's mine." "Thank you baby." She said kissing him again. Her and Zander got comfy on the couch and held hands. She laid her head on his shoulder and he kissed the top of her head.

"It's that going to be a little weird?" Whispered Jordan. "Not really. She's only sleeping with me. They both have been through so much. As long as they're happy, I'm happy. He whispered back.

He started making breakfast. Pancakes, bacon, and sausage. Then he poured everyone some orange juice. "Breakfast is ready," he yelled. They all sat at the kitchen table. He grabbed Lila's face and kissed her deep. She kissed him back passionately. Zander was sitting next to her and squeezed her leg. He squeezed him back reassuring him.

"Ok you two let us eat in peace." Said Jordan. They stopped kissing and ate their food. "This is so good. Thank you baby." "Anything for you princess." They finished eating. "It's supposed to be nice out today. Can we sit outside?" Asked Lila. "That sounds good." Said Benjie.

They went outside together. Lila sat between Zander and Alex. Alex held her hand but Zander gave them some space. Jordan brought them out some sodas. Lila smiled and thanked him. They enjoyed just relaxing in the sun. Lila was in a pretty sunflower dress. The rest of the boys were shirtless with shorts on. A few women in bikinis walked by catching their attention. Alex and Zander didn't pay them any mind but the other two winked at them. Alex squeezed her hand and smiled at her.

A little time went by and Alex had to pee. "I'll be back my love." He said kissing her. Jordan and Benjie went out to the main beach to go find some girls. As soon as Alex was inside, Zander held her hand and pulled her face in for a kiss. He behaved tho and kissed her on the cheek. She kissed him back.

Alex ended up having to poop instead. He texted Lila. I got to poop. No kissing you two. She typed back. I'll behave, don't worry. He answered You better or I'll spank you. She responded ☺

"He's got to poop." "That's great I can spend more time alone with you." "Yes but we gotta behave." "Let's take a walk on the beach." They walked hand in hand. The hot sand getting in their sandals. She saw some seashells lying by the shore. "Oh these are pretty." She said bending down to pick them up. He bent down next to her and started picking some up too. Jordan and Benjie noticed them. "I know he doesn't want to lose her but eventually I feel like him and Zander are going to get really jealous of each other." Said Benjie. "I don't know. I just hope no one gets hurt." Said Jordan. They looked into each other's eyes. They wanted to kiss each other so bad but they were loyal to Alex.

He kissed her cheek a few times. She blushed and gave him a hug. She lost her balance though and fell butt first into the sand.

They both laughed and he helped her up. He started brushing the sand off of her dress but by this time Alex was coming up behind them. "She fell in the sand and nothing happened." He said nervously. He playfully spanked her butt and giggled. "I told you not to bed a bad girl." "I wasn't, I wasn't." She said, "Alex pulled her close and kissed her while squeezing her butt. She spanked him back. "You are a bad girl!" She took off for the water and ran in till the water was at her waist. All the boys followed her in. "Water feels so nice." "Yes it is my baby." He said moving closer to her. Zander splashed them. "Ha ha you can't catch me." He said teasing them. Lila splashed him and then he jumped on both on them in the water.

"You are in trouble now." Said Alex. He tackled him and Lila tackled Alex. Alex got up and kissed her while she was floating in the water. Zander decided to be naughty while they were kissing and splashed them. Alex stopped kissing her and splashed him back. He could sense that her and Zander really wanted to play with each other in the water but he was trusting them to behave. They locked eyes with each other. She started getting emotional. She couldn't shake this feeling she had for him. He looked at Alex as if to ask for permission to comfort her.

He nodded with approval. He went over and hugged her in the water. "Don't cry beautiful, I'm here." "But I want to kiss you and I can't. What is wrong with me? Falling in love with two people. I'm a tramp." Alex went over to comfort her. Zander stepped back. "You can stay." Said Alex. "There's nothing wrong with you. You just have a big heart. That's something I love about you." "Let's just get some so you can dry off and calm down. Who do you want to walk you home?" Asked Alex. "Both of you."

Chapter 9: A Tragic Wedding

Six more months went by and soon they had been together for a year. They were all set to get married. Alex had bought Sarah a plane ticket so she could be there when the time came. Sadly a paparazzi broke the news of the upcoming wedding to a tabloid. So it was all over the Internet. They couldn't change the date though because they had made all the reservations and paid the deposits. It was going to be a beachfront wedding.

They couldn't wait to get married. Zander was still a little jealous but was happy that he could still have Lila in his life. The band mates were busy getting Alex ready while Sarah was there to help Lila. Everything was already set up at the beach. The chairs, flowers and they had yummy food that was going to be delivered post wedding.

"I can't believe you are getting married." "Me either!" She started curling her hair with a curling iron. Her gorgeous white dress was already on. "I'm so glad you found happiness. You deserve it." "Thank you, I hope you find your prince charming someday too." They both smiled at each other.

Soon she finished getting her ready. She looked beautiful. Zander came up dressed sharply in a black suit and purple tie. "Ready for me to walk you down the aisle?" He asked kissing her cheek. "Yes I am." They linked arms and the three of them started walking towards the beach. An elegant wedding arch made with pink flowers stood at the edge of the beach. Alex was in a blue suede suit and he looked stunning. Everyone watched as Lila and Zander walked down the aisle. Sarah took her place in front of the arch and was getting teary eyed. Zander hugged Lila and whispered that he loved her. She said she loved him back. Then he stood by Sarah and started crying himself.

"Dearly beloved, we are gathered here today to join Alexander and Lila in holy matrimony. Alex do you take Lila to be your wife in sickness and health till death do you part? "I do." "Lila do you take Alex to be your husband in sickness and health till death do you part? "I do." "I now pronounce you husband and wife. You may kiss." "Ah that man has a gun!" Someone shouted. They turned around in horror to see Mark pointing a pistol right at Lila. "You are going to die." He shouted. He fired the gun but Zander jumped in front of her just as Benjie tackled Mark. The bullet went through him and punchered his heart. He fell to the ground and was bleeding heavily. Someone dialed 911 to help Zander and take Mark to jail but it looked like Zander wasn't going to make it.

Alex and Lila started crying and holding their hands on his chest to stop the bleeding but it was no use. "Lila I love you." She bent down and kissed his lips one last time. "I love you too." She wept. "I love you too my brother." He said hugging him. "I love you too.

The ambulance arrived but it was too late. Lila laid on his chest crying hysterically. Alex rubbed her back and tried to calm her. The police dragged Mark off after tasering him. He was to be locked up for life.

Chapter 10: Epilogue

It had been a year after Zander had past. Lila and Alex were pregnant with their first child. They were having a boy. That day they were visiting Zander's grave. Lila bent down and placed a bouquet of flowers. Then she kissed his gravestone. "I miss you so much. I'm having a boy and I'm naming him after you. I love you so much." "I love you too my brother. We will see you someday."

Don't miss out!

Visit the website below and you can sign up to receive emails whenever Skye Rickman publishes a new book. There's no charge and no obligation.

https://books2read.com/r/B-A-CYAQB-IESND

BOOKS 2 READ

Connecting independent readers to independent writers.

About the Author

Skye is a young woman from New York who enjoys horror and romance movies. She has had a passion for writing since she was 16. She loves all things fantasy and paranormal. You can find all her information on her Kofi page. There you can purchase books and more.